VIRAL LIVES

A Ghost Story

Written by FELIX I.D. DIMARO

Cover Artwork by Rosco Nischler

Typography and Graphic Design by Courtney Swank

Copyright @2020 FELIX I.D. DIMARO

ALSO BY
FELIX I.D. DIMARO

How To Make A Monster:
The Loveliest Shade of Red

Bug Spray:
A Tale of Madness

This story contains mature content, including explicit language, violence, and sexual subject matter.

For everyone with
a secret they hope
is never revealed.

CHAPTER ONE

Sometimes, people just want to watch other people die.

It was as simple as that to Simon Hinch. As simple as him delivering a service to many people who yearned for it. People who needed it. What would these people do if he and others like him didn't do what they did? He often rationalized this to himself. Rationalized to the point that he considered what he did to be hero's work. A valuable service.

Simon believed he was giving these people something that, if not for him and others like him, they might have gone out and sought for themselves. And that would be no good. That would be an ugly thing. With that in mind, Simon considered what he did to be heroic in a sense. Which is why, when he heard the sound of screeching tires, followed by a violent crash, another crash immediately after, and then a thud, he smiled. And went to do his duty.

Simon was on a bicycle. That was how he travelled around Saturn City on his missions, looking for things to film, to sell, to upload. That was the convenient way, he'd found, for him to access the carnage in this city, and to exit from that carnage undetected.

A car wouldn't have allowed him to weave through the tight areas of Saturn City, cutting through the litter strewn alleyways and backlots full of homeless lives that society had forgotten. If he had been in a car, he may not have heard the source of all of those wonderful sounds he had just heard. And had he been on foot, he might not have been able to get there as quickly as he wound up getting there. That would have meant missing the magic moment. The only moment that mattered.

Simon pedaled down an alleyway, his tires zipping through puddles and leaving trails of sprayed water as he made his way through the freshly rained upon city. He ended up on a sidewalk facing what would typically be one of the busiest streets this far south in Saturn: Coal Town Road.

It was approaching 4 AM, and most of the city was asleep. Simon knew this. What he depended upon were the people who lived in the night. The people who, at ungodly hours such as this, would be leaving the illegal sporting books and casinos, the afterhours clubs, the 24/7 diners. What he depended upon were the people who looked for a good time every time, with no time designated for time off.

The dregs of society. The drug dependant, the utterly irresponsible. This was who he sought.

And here was one of them, he presumed.

Simon only wished he had been there even a minute earlier. It's not likely that he would have been able to film the crash, or gotten his camera out in time for him to capture this person (who was now dragging his body through the street) at the moment he had flown through the windshield. But he would have caught more of the aftermath.

Fans of the sort of work Simon was involved in loved to hear the struggle. The noises. The exclamations of pain. The cries for all matter of unattainable things, the first of which was usually help.

But it was the death rattles, Simon knew, that made for lots of views, which made for lots of dollars. Any video where someone could be heard struggling to breathe, gurgling while dying. That sold like gold.

He had never personally captured the magic moment. He hoped that would change immediately. Right now. This would be the first real chance. This would be his big break.

Leaving his bike at the mouth of the alleyway after making sure that the street was relatively empty and that no one might interfere, Simon approached the crawling man on foot. He removed his phone from his fanny pack, turned on the video function and hit the record button.

He aimed the camera to the right, first capturing the wreckage of the car. It had crashed into a hydro pole with such force that the pole had nearly been uprooted and was now sitting slightly askew, conjoined to the small sedan at its base. The passenger side of that vehicle was wrapped around the pole, the driver's side was malformed, the windshield shattered open, smoke rose from beneath its crumpled hood. A trail of blood led from the car – and Simon carefully panned across this trail of blood – to the victim, the unfortunate man who was crawling senselessly somewhere, nowhere. Dying. Calling out,

"Help!" A gasp. A wheeze. But Simon heard it clearly in the empty street as he approached the victim. Simon went to him, not to help the man, but to help himself.

He knew he had to be quick. Understood that, with a crash that loud, and with this many buildings around, there was bound to be someone watching, witnessing, filming. Though he was confident that these people wouldn't call for help, because, in a place like this, calling for help only meant harassment. These people would watch until they became bored, then they would return to their beds or wherever they lurked during this time of day that was neither day or night, allowing things to sort themselves out.

This was the way of Saturn City. Simon had seen it play out a thousand times. Knew that someone could be observing no matter how quiet or desolate an area seemed. Which is why he dressed in a way he believed gave him anonymity. To any onlookers, he was simply a cyclist dressed in a nondescript long sleeve jersey and padded bib pants. One who wore a helmet for safety and a balaclava over his face to, they would assume, protect himself from the cool winds as he rode around town. But all of this was to ensure his privacy. To make certain he never wound up in the spotlight.

Simon had seen videos of himself online a time or two. More aptly, he had seen himself in videos featuring other people as the focal point. Videos involving fights, instances of violence, films of the misfortunes of others. Each time he had spotted himself doing his own recording in these recordings, he was certain he wouldn't be able to be identified, and he wanted to keep it that way. Because there is always an eye or two or few, watching. Witnessing. Some cyclopean eye somewhere seizing secrets with its lens.

Simon had made his way in front of this man who was dragging his damaged body through the empty street, giving him a space of fifteen feet or so. He was capturing the crawling creature head on. Simon was thrilled (though he would never use this word to describe it) by what he was seeing.

The man was a wreck. Nearly as damaged as the wreckage of the vehicle he had exited abruptly. It was a surprise, to Simon, that the man was able to move at all. He was dragging himself, closing the gap between them, seeming to move on pure instinct and nervous reaction. Simon thought of a chicken with its head cut off, running around for seconds before realizing it was dead. This is what this man reminded him of, and it gave Simon a small sense of relief to know that the man was beyond help. He would be on his way to whatever was on the other side whether or not Simon was standing there recording. This was another of Simon's rationalizations. He was simply just an observer and recorder of the inevitable.

Most of the man's face was shredded or peeled away; there were flaps of skin hanging from his cheeks. His face, to Simon, brought about images of the display behind a butcher shop window. A shard of glass was stuck either directly in or immediately beside the man's left eye. The eye itself was blacked out by blood.

His right eye was bloodshot and vacant, scanning but not quite registering his surroundings. His lips were in several pieces, as though the man had attempted to kiss the blades of a running meat grinder. Passionately. Simon only had to raise his camera back to the damaged car for a moment to see the windshield, a hole punched through it where the body had exited. A jagged hole, all red coated sharp edges like the mouth of a shark after taking a bite out of some unlucky swimmer.

And here was this unfortunate man, crawling away as if seeking the safety of an unseen shore. One that would forever be beyond him.

Then the man released a sound. A death gurgle. It seemed to come from his throat where Simon could see a large, leaking laceration.

Perfect, Simon thought. *Absolutely perfect.* People liked to see other people die, but hearing the process made it real. Made the experience that much more personal.

Then there came another sound, and this made Simon think of Christmas come early. He could hardly believe it, but the man was still trying, and able – just barely – to talk.

Through a torn and shredded face, this bleeding, dying, tattered man said,

"You... Help..." He croaked the words out, looking up at Simon through one barely open eye. "Please. Help me..."

Simon said nothing, but he thought many things in that moment as his heart thrashed against his breastbone. This was the closest to death he had ever been. All of the videos, all of the photos he had viewed online, all of the bloody brawls he had witnessed personally, even the aftermath of accidents where he had managed to capture a photo or two of a dead body from afar, none of it was this.

This was Death in the process of being. Of taking. This was the Reaper in the middle of his harvest. Simon watched, and as a few more gurgles escaped the man's mouth and neck, Simon thought:

I am *helping you.*

He thought:

You don't know it, but I'm giving you your fifteen minutes of fame. That's what everyone wants.

Simon silently projected these thoughts at the man as he also rationalized his actions to himself. He wanted to say it all out loud but knew he couldn't risk having his voice on the recording. It had to be clean. Only the death noises. He couldn't taint those with his excitement.

You're going to go out as a celebrity, my good man. In a way, you'll be around forever, a never dying viral you. That's all the help you're gonna get. As if he could read the thoughts Simon was projecting toward him, the tattered man looked up with his one good eye, the one which seemed, to Simon, to be glazed over. Seemed to be looking through Simon and not directly at him. Simon saw everything inside of that eye very clearly as he searched for the one thing that would make this video perfect. The one thing that would make him thousands of dollars.

He was looking for the moment.

The magic moment. The only moment that truly mattered to this dying man, to everyone, eventually.

Then he saw it.

Something inside of that eye faded, grayed, dulled, died. The rest of the tattered man followed suit once the life had departed from his eye. He fell flat, his head hitting the road with an echoing thud. Simon knew the viewers would love that too.

Perfect, he thought, not for the first or last time regarding this man's death. *Absolutely perfect.* Then he turned off and put away his phone before sprinting back to his bicycle. Simon jumped on the bike and pumped the pedals as fast as he could, listening for sirens but not expecting to hear any. Not in a place like this. Still, he flew through the streets back to his apartment, fueled by his elation, the broad smile on his face rubbing against the mask that covered it. He couldn't believe his luck. He had managed to capture the moment the life had left a person's body, soul squeezed out by Death's hard hands. Such a rarity.

Simon couldn't wait to get home. He pedalled harder than he ever had before, eager to sit down and watch what he had just recorded.

CHAPTER TWO

Simon watched the video several times after uploading it from his phone to his laptop, his delight never dimming all the while.

The sun was rising, the new light bleeding through the cracks of the blinds that blocked his view from the balcony as he sat at his kitchen table. He had done a celebratory line of cocaine and a shot of whiskey not long after his arrival. He wanted to stay up and wait for a response from his usual buyer.

This was money in the bank.

He clicked replay. Stared unblinking. Clicked replay again. Again. More. He watched repeatedly as the eye within the tattered face of a dying man lost its shine, stared at least a dozen times as it lost that light right after looking in a glazed sort of way at the camera. Heard those death gurgles, saw and heard the man's head drop to the ground, soulless. This was, to Simon, like seeing art in motion.

Did he feel guilt? Perhaps at one point he had, but over time Simon had come to understand that this part-time profession of his was a job just like any other. There was a demand, and he was one of the people bold enough to meet it.

He considered himself a Gore Reporter. Simply an amateur journalist documenting the darker side of humanity, the things the mainstream media tried to shield people from, as though humans haven't been seeing and seeking grisly morbid sights for centuries. There's a reason traffic slows even after freshly crashed cars are taken off the road.

It was Simon's belief that the human mind contains within it a naturally morbid curiosity which yearns to be fed. And here he was, ready to dish out an item that would satiate the ravenous desires of many.

What he hoped, each time he was out in the streets ready to press record or take a photo, was to document the most natural and inevitable part of life – the end of it. He didn't wish for people to die, that would be wrong, but he knew that people did that inexorable thing, and somewhat frequently. He only wanted to be around to document it. To document the one thing each and every person is curious about, and something that so many people thirst to see, if only to witness death and feel some sort of unrecognized pride because they are still living and breathing and carrying on. Watching death, Simon knew, made people feel more alive. And, in this moment, repeatedly going over the video of a man's last breath, he felt as alive as he had ever felt before.

He felt no conflict. Was free of internal strife. Simon didn't feel bad because he knew people did what he was paid to do for free, just out of genuine curiosity and the need to appease that same curiosity in others. These people diminished his work by sharing and viewing their minor gore stories on Facebook and Instagram and YouTube, relishing every neutered clip of someone's personal mishap, seeking out any police brutality video they could find, often disguising their sadism as social justice. As a need – a responsibility, some would convince themselves – to be aware of what was going on in the world.

There had been a time when people could only see these sorts of videos on the gore sites. Now, violent videos were everywhere, though usually watered down, the bloody bits blurred. As if people could only handle the gore they thirsted for in sips rather than the full swallows they desired and deserved. Simon believed that people should be able to consume as they wanted, and as often as they wanted.

This was what made his job important. It was raw. It was real. It was giving the people what they wanted to consume.

He had found a true gem on this early morning. Had found something that people would have to seek out especially. Something the mainstream media would never risk their reputations to show. And, if they did, the entire video would be a muted blur.

There was so much blood.

He clicked replay again. Watched that one reddened eye blinking away its life, staring foggily through the lens and at the people who would eventually view this footage. The sponsors would eat it up, drink it down. Simon considered it a job well done.

His phone buzzed, vibrating loudly against the faux wood dining table, surprising him and giving him a jolt. He checked it excitedly and was glad to see that it was his buyer, awake an hour before expected.

Simon had sent him an email containing a brief and coded description of what he had to offer not long after his bump of coke and shot of whiskey. And had set his asking price higher than he ever had before. He was expecting some pushback, bargaining, haggling. So, when he picked up his phone, opened the email from the person who went by Mr. Rood, and saw the response agreeing to his request, Simon got up and did a little dance of joy.

Life had never felt so good.

CHAPTER THREE

The video was uploaded to thegorereport.com even before the man's death had been reported on the news. Simon wondered vaguely, after finally spotting the report of the fatal one-vehicle collision on a standard news website later that morning, if the dead man's next of kin had been made aware of his fate before the gore hounds on the web had seen the video.

The footage had been made public an hour before Simon had spotted that first news article reporting the man's death, approximately half an hour after nearly six months' rent had been transferred into Simon's bank account by Mr. Rood.

Almost immediately the comments had rolled in:

'That fucking gurgle! OMG!'

'You can see that he knew he was dying. Like you can see him seeing his soul leaving his body. Fuuuuuck that's intense!'

'I'm pretty sure that's his Adam's Apple there showing through the slash in his neck. How is he still talking? What a trooper.'

'Fuck this. It's fake. No way someone was right there at the moment of death, and this guy just happened to know to look dramatically into the camera before dying? Fake news. I expect better Gore Report!'

Simon clicked on that last comment and saw, with a small measure of delight, that at least a dozen people had defended the veracity of the video. Some chastising the original commenter for not knowing what a real dying person looked like. Most defending the honour of The Gore Report.

Traffic. His video was creating traffic. He grinned pridefully at this.

After an hour of scrolling through the comments and watching the views grow, Simon was nearly ready to go to bed.

His phone buzzed against the table again. It was close to 10 AM on Saturday morning, and he knew who it would be immediately. It was a message he received each morning, and a message he had been waiting for since he'd received confirmation of the money in his account. He read the 'Good morning' text with a small smile. Now drained of the exhilaration from that morning, Simon had just enough energy to deliver this long overdue bit of good news. And he wanted to do it over the phone properly, not via text.

"Hey babe. How was your shift?" came the freshly woken voice of Simon's girlfriend, Jayne Correa, after she'd answered his call nearly immediately.

"Best shift I've had in a while," he said truthfully, the happy clear in his voice. "I'm going to send you a link. Call me back after you check it out." He disconnected the call and sent Jayne the link to the most recent video uploaded to The Gore Report's feature page.

It didn't take Jayne long to call back, the sleep knocked right out of her voice. She sounded as excited he felt.

"Jesus Christ, Simon, you really got this on video? Have you seen the comments?"

The smile on Simon's face seeped into his words as he responded.

"Can you believe it?" he asked. "I never really expected this to happen. And Rood gave me exactly what I asked for. And I asked for a lot. I was expecting him to bargain but he didn't even hesitate. You know what this means?"

"No... What does it mean?" she asked, her voice made up of nervous wonder.

"We can finally take that trip to Jamaica we've been talking about forever."

She responded to this the way he had expected her to. High pitched notes of excitement. Immediately going into planning mode: when, which city, which resort. The sorts of things she had been hoping they could talk about for far too long.

Simon and Jayne had been together for over two years and had yet to take a proper vacation anywhere. Part of the reason Simon had started prowling the rough neighbourhoods at night looking to capture and sell images of people in unfortunate situations was because neither he nor Jayne had great day jobs, and they always found themselves struggling just to make ends meet.

He wanted to propose to her, had wanted to for some time. And now, with this influx of money, he could do it while on vacation. He knew she wasn't expecting it at all. Had no clue he had been saving for a ring for over a year. That morning's footage would help him procure the perfect diamond. Simon couldn't remember the last time he'd been this excited. Never would have imagined himself even considering marriage, and here he was, preparing a proposal.

The reason Jayne had turned out to be the one, when Simon had always had options for many, was because of days like today. He could share with her what he did with his late nights and, not only did she not judge him, she trusted him. That's what he loved most about Jayne, just how trusting she was. That level of trust was exactly what a man like Simon needed in a partner. For a variety of reasons.

"Okay, okay, okay." he said to her, his voice still full of his smile. "I have to get to bed. We still on for tonight?"

They were. Simon disconnected the call. Looking forward to the wild night that would take place after his regularly scheduled date night with Jayne, he went to bed and quickly fell asleep with a grin still on his face.

CHAPTER FOUR

"You sure you can't stay over?" Simon asked sweetly from the bed, watching Jayne look all over his bedroom for one article of clothing or the next. Clothing which had been ripped off and strewn all over the bedroom as they had rushed there after returning from the Italian restaurant and sci-fi movie she had chosen for this iteration of date night.

"You know I *want* to stay over, but I can't." she said, pausing her search to look at him. He could see that it pained her to say that sentence, especially with all of the excitement between them since they now had something more to look forward to other than the mundanity of the regular routine they had fallen into over the last year of their relationship.

"I have to be up before the sun, and you practically just woke up for the day. Besides," Jayne said with a playful smirk, "I need all the beauty sleep I can get for our vacation."

Their vacation had been the topic of conversation for most of the night, though neither of them felt it necessary to talk about the man who had died and made their upcoming trip a possibility. Simon wouldn't have minded if the discussion had gone that way, but he knew Jayne. While she didn't judge him, she would let guilt seep into her mind if they dwelled on the subject for too long. Simon was perfectly fine with avoiding the topic of the star of his recording, thinking it might be better to ignore the fact that some unfortunate dead guy had been responsible for making his marriage proposal possible. It wasn't exactly something he could bring up in his speech at the wedding.

"I wish you had better hours." he said sincerely.

After jumping up and down and squeezing herself into the ultra tight jeans she had worn that evening, Jayne looked at him with mock exasperation, rolling her eyes to indicate they had talked about this many times before. Jayne was the assistant manager at Fred's Renovation and Landscaping. A position she had worked her way up to over years. One that required her to open the store at ungodly hours five days a week, and, too often, at least one of those days landed on the weekend. She had already told him she was dreading the thirty-minute drive to the sprawling store in the way-too-early Sunday morning gloom.

"It'll be worth the wait, I promise," she said, her voice muffled as her sweater made its way over her face. "I'm off all weekend next weekend, remember? I'll be all yours after the party on Saturday."

"Ugh." Simon uttered. "You sure we can't skip that and get straight back to this?"

"I think my sister would be pretty pissed at me if we did that." she said, laughing. Then walked over and gave him a kiss while pulling him out of the bed. "Walk me to the door."

"You kiss me like that and expect me *not* to beg you to stay over?"

"Gotta give you something to look forward to all week. Other than the party, of course."

Next week's event was not something Simon was looking forward to whatsoever. He avoided events such as these as much as he could with his own family, but always wound up being dragged to gatherings held by Jayne's family and friends.

"Alright. Just remember your promise. Saturday night better be worth the wait." he responded playfully. She assured him that it would be, and, before she left, Jayne gave him one final lingering kiss.

He closed the door behind her. While he was looking forward to the following Saturday night far more than he had been before, he wasn't quite through with this Saturday yet.

Tracking down his phone, Simon sent a text message to someone who was eagerly waiting to hear from him. It read:

Hey. I'll be there as soon as I can.

He waited for the response. Smirked when he received it. Then he proceeded to hurry into the shower, still not quite believing how great this weekend was turning out to be.

CHAPTER FIVE

Less than an hour later, a freshly showered, smugly smiling Simon was standing in front of a door belonging to a modest bungalow in a quiet neighbourhood, waiting to be invited in.

When the door opened, his expression changed to one of ravenous greed. Sheer want. She never ceased to wow him, the woman that was standing there, enjoying the look of naked approval on Simon's face. Approval of her nakedness.

The door had been opened by a woman who wore nothing but a smile.

Simon looked down at her torso and saw three large, beautiful, engorged mounds, each of them driving him instantly wild.

She was pregnant. The fact that the baby didn't belong to him was the best part of this scenario to Simon. The father of the baby – her husband – was out of town on a business trip. He was out of town at least once a month, and these two took full advantage of his excursions each time. Something about that, about their entire secret situation, drove him wild in a way that Jayne – even though she could deal with his part-time occupation as a Gore Reporter – could never understand. He loved Jayne, but love sometimes grew boring. Mundane. The sex he'd just had with Jayne a couple of hours ago had been fine. Just fine. But not much more than that. Simon was okay with mediocre relationship sex. Was genuinely looking forward to marrying Jayne and having that same mediocre sex for the rest of their lives. He would remain okay with it because he knew where to get what he needed, when he needed it, elsewhere.

What Simon needed was what was in front of him now. Something that would be more than just fine. What he needed was unbridled lust, ever aflame.

She pulled him in. No words, just motion.

He kissed her the way he had kissed Jayne earlier when he had been thinking about this pregnant woman he now held. He let her guide him into her den, where he saw that the coffee table had been moved out of the way, and a layer of plastic sheeting had been spread all over the carpeted floor.

This, he thought, looking at the display impatiently, was the perfect way to celebrate all that had gone right for him that weekend.

She let him set up his phone from a vantage where the entire scene could be captured. It wasn't the first time he had filmed this illicit act of theirs. There was trust between them. Trust in the potential for mutual destruction. Each of them knew their secret was safe with the other. Had been for some time.

Finally, he undressed and went to her.

Simon stayed there for hours doing things they would never dare describe to anyone other than each other. Private perversions. Dirty secrets.

He drank of her, and she of him. And, when they had sufficiently drained each other, he kissed her pregnant stomach goodbye and walked in a daze from her house to the Uber waiting for him half a block down her street. The entire way to the vehicle he felt like he was walking on a cloud, the ninth nimbus.

This has gotta be the best weekend I've ever had, Simon thought to himself drunkenly, not solely from the alcohol he had consumed throughout the evening and night, but mostly from his mistress. Simon remained on cloud nine the entire drive home. Stayed there until he drifted off of that cloud onto his bed and floated into sleep.

CHAPTER SIX

Sleep didn't stay for long that early Sunday morning. Simon's phone wouldn't allow it.

Shortly after coming home from his mistress's house, stumbling into bed and into a blissful sleep, his alarm clock had gone off. Blaring and braying unbidden.

He reached out, fumbling for his phone on his nightstand before finding it and turning off the alarm.

Simon was irritated and confused. He squinted at the overbright screen of his mobile device and saw that it was 3:50 AM. He often set his alarm for odd times when he planned to cruise around the city looking for material, but never on a Sunday, nor at this time when it was both too early and too late to set out and find anything of significance. After double-checking that there weren't any other accidental alarms set, Simon was once again able to go to sleep.

The moment he had drifted into sleep, the alarm sounded again pulling him out of his slumber. He grunted in frustration at his phone and reached for it again. Again turning off the alarm. Once more making sure there were no other accidental alarms set. This time he put the phone into the drawer of his nightstand instead of atop it. Just in case. And, after a few minutes of doing his best to swallow the frustration he had at his mobile device, he was able to fall asleep for the third time.

The alarm blared as soon as he had fallen asleep, wailing like a foghorn from inside of the drawer. Illogically loud. Much louder than it should have been.

"What the fuck, you stupid fucking piece of useless shit!" he screamed, half into his pillow and half in the direction of the phone. He immediately felt foolish for lashing out, hoping that the neighbours hadn't heard him through the too-thin walls.

"Christ. What is wrong with this thing?" he asked no one.

Simon grabbed the phone from the drawer, turning off the alarm again, turning off the phone entirely this time as well.

He placed it back in the drawer. Burrowed his frustrated face into his pillow.

Ten minutes later, he was asleep.

Eleven minutes later, his phone began braying again.

"Fuuuuuck!" he whispered harshly, reaching into the drawer and grabbing the phone. He was ready to turn it off once again but saw that it was already powered down, the alarm no longer sounding. His face slacked with his surprise and confusion. He went to turn on the phone in order to see if he could figure out the malfunction, cursing the phone's manufacturer under his breath. Cursing a little louder when the device wouldn't turn on. He swore again as he fumbled in the dark for the power cord that was usually on his nightstand, assuming the phone's battery must have died.

"Alexa. Turn on the bedroom lights." Simon said to the household electronic assistant that took care of most of the things he didn't feel like reaching for or typing out.

The lights remined off. Alexa didn't respond.

"Alexa..." he said, wondering if maybe the power had gone out. "Turn on the bedroom lights."

Nothing.

Simon got up out of bed, walked half-asleep and fully annoyed toward the light switch, cursing Alexa as he had done his phone while he did so.

He reached the light switch. Flipped it up. On. But the lights didn't respond.

Simon opened his bedroom door, still holding his dead phone in his hand.

"Alexa," he decided to try again. "Turn on the living room lights." And this time something happened, though it wasn't the something he expected.

As he gazed into the living area of his apartment, able to see both the living room and the kitchen of the open concept unit, three things turned on. None of them were the lights.

The phone vibrated in his hand. The shock of this feeling caused him to drop it on the floor. Cursing again, he quickly stooped over to pick it up, but what he saw on the screen made him recoil.

The phone had not only turned on, but it was playing the recording of the dying man that had given his weekend and his future such a boost. There was no sound playing along with the video.

Simon recovered from his shock, picked up his phone, went to turn the recording off but then he noticed a light shining somewhere in the darkness of his apartment. He looked up and saw that his television was on. He nearly fell over when he saw what it displayed. The video, the same footage of the crawling, dying, face-torn man, was playing on his television.

"What the..." Simon whispered to himself. Then, before he panicked, he realized he must have linked the video from his phone to his television somehow. He quickly had another realization: the power couldn't be out if the TV was on.

"Alexa, turn off the TV."

Nothing happened. Simon, exasperated at this point, walked into the living room, to his coffee table where the remote control for the television lay. He grabbed it, went to turn off the television, and that's when he noticed that his laptop on the kitchen table was also on. He was certain he had turned it off, certain too that it had been a black screen when he had walked out of his bedroom. Yet there it was, glowing in the dim; it too playing the video of the tattered man crawling nowhere but to Death.

Simon looked from his laptop to his television to his phone. Each screen was playing the video, all of them in sync. His eyes settled on the television, the largest of the three screens, the remote control for it was still in his hand. He saw the same footage he had watched dozens of times since recording it. Watched the man crawl, witnessed him leak, so much of his skin turned to flapping ribbons in the fall breeze.

Yet he continued to crawl, to look up at Simon. Each of the devices was muted, so Simon couldn't hear the gurgling sound he had heard the man make from the hole in this throat as he had tried to ask for help. And, for the first time, Simon was grateful for that. All at once he had a bad feeling about everything going on around him.

"Alexa, turn on the living room light... Turn on the kitchen light."

Not a single light responded to the commands. He remained in darkness other than the luminance emitting from his several screens.

He went over to the light switch in the living room, tried to turn the light on manually. Nothing happened. He pointed the remote control at the television and attempted to shut it off, not wanting to watch this silent film in the dark.

The television remained on.

Bewildered, Simon turned his attention to his phone. Tried to disconnect the link sending the footage from the mobile device to the TV, but the video would not minimize from the screen.

Nor would it pause.

Nor would it stop.

He attempted to power down the cell phone. Much like the television, it remained on, both devices still playing the movie he had made. Except, the longer the video played the more wrong it became. The man in the recording was still crawling, though Simon was sure that, at this point in the video, he had collapsed and died. Yet now, on all three screens he continued to crawl. Closer. So close to the camera. Too close.

He should have stopped by now, Simon thought. Then his thoughts paused as he watched the man drag his dying body even nearer to the camera. For a terrifying and irrational moment, Simon was worried the man would crawl straight through the screen and break into this world.

No, he thought. *No. This doesn't happen in real life.* He convinced himself he was dreaming. Living some walking nightmare.

He threw his phone on the couch, making sure the screen was facing down. He ran to his laptop and closed it. The entire time he was doing this, Simon pressed on the remote control in his hand. Hit the power button so many useless times. The television would not turn off.

He ran to the TV, calling for Alexa to shut it off, asking the machine to turn on the lights. Alternating between these requests as the broken body on his television crept closer and closer to the screen. Impossibly close. Not what he had recorded.

When he got to the television, just as he was about to hit the power button, the TV turned off. The lights turned on. Simon breathed a shaky sigh of relief, his body trembling wildly.

Just a glitch, he thought.

"Thank you, Alexa." Simon whispered, relief and scorn both in his voice.

In response, the speakers that usually projected Alexa's feminine but robotic voice made a noise unlike any he had ever heard from them.

The speakers emitted that sound just as all of the lights turned off again.

It was a gurgling noise, like someone choking, like someone desperate. Dying. It was the sound of the tattered man.

And it sounded like he was everywhere.

To Simon, standing in the absolute dark, it sounded like that dying man was near. Right next to him. So close that Simon believed he could smell his bloody breath.

And that's when Simon decided he no longer wanted to be in his apartment.

CHAPTER SEVEN

Simon moved as quickly as he could in the blackness of his unit. Stumbling here, tripping there, feeling around for anything that might impede him as he made his way directly from his living room to the front door. He opened it and was grateful to see that the hallway was lit. Whatever was causing the malfunction of the lights in his apartment wasn't happening out here.

He turned toward the stairs and began to run, not sure where he was going, only knowing he had to get away from that sound. From that darkness.

He made it several paces down the hallway before he regained his senses enough to remember what he was wearing. What he wore to bed every night. Nothing.

Simon looked down at his naked body in the bright hallway. He looked up at all the doors, so many doors, any of which could open at any time. He turned and began to quickly walk back to his apartment, reasoning with himself with each step. Telling himself it was too much coke, too much whisky and milk, too much excitement for one weekend. His overstimulated mind must have just exaggerated a few technological glitches.

With each step, he rationalized, convinced himself, reassured himself that he was being silly.

When Simon re-entered the apartment, the lights were on and the television was off. He was thankful for both.

After hesitantly closing and locking the door, he, very slowly, carefully, as if worried it might detonate upon his touch, walked toward the phone he had left on the couch.

Picked it up. It was on and, thankfully, the video was no longer playing on the screen.

The first thing he did was look for the footage on his phone and delete it. He had saved it on his laptop, and he could visit The Gore Report if he ever needed to see it again. The video would be out there forever. The late-night reminders of it from a glitching phone wouldn't be necessary.

Understanding that he had a long night ahead of him even though it would be day in only a matter of hours, Simon turned off his phone and left it on his coffee table. Although they were now off, he avoided looking at his television and his laptop as he returned to his bedroom.

From a box in his closet, Simon retrieved one of the few books he had in his home – a battered copy of George Orwell's 1984, which he had failed to both read and return to his English class during his last year of High School nearly a decade prior. He went to bed preparing to read for the first time in years.

With every light in his apartment on, Simon read while waiting for daylight, or sleep. Whichever came first.

CHAPTER EIGHT

Daylight came first. Sleep followed shortly thereafter. Simon fell asleep with his book on his face and his mind full of dark thoughts.

He dreamt of being underwater. Swimming. He was a shark in this dream. Powerful and dangerous, at least at first. But, whenever he tried to swim out further into the depths of the ocean, he was stopped by some invisible barrier. He kept trying to swim, but kept being stopped.

Suddenly he understood he was in an aquarium, not in the ocean where he belonged. He understood this not only because of the glass that stopped him from moving forward, but because there were people there watching him struggle to swim. Small people. Children. Each of them with bloody faces distorted by the water Simon peered through in order to see them.

All of them stood, pointed, laughed as they bled from their eyes. Their chortles warped and warbling as the sound travelled through the water. They laughed like children would if no adult had given them a single lesson in morality. Laughed like those who have never been instructed that laughing at the plight of others is the incorrect thing to do. Even when it is only a witless animal being mocked.

That is how they laughed as Simon continued to thrash about, desperately looking for a way out. It was then he noticed that he was shrinking. The more they took their joy of him, the smaller he became, until he was no longer a shark but a minnow. A minnow surrounded by giant, distorted, bloody faces, all of them cackling in that twisted malicious way only children can, taking delight in his misery. Simon went to scream at them, to urge them to stop, but underwater he could make no sound.

He woke up wet. Drenched in nightmare sweat. The book which had rested on his face as he fell to sleep was now pasted there with perspiration. In Simon's panic he thought the tome was some sea creature attempting to attack him. He hurled it off his forehead, launching it all the way across the room, and only awoke fully when it clanged against the wall, then the floor. Each solid sound bringing him closer to reality.

He was discombobulated, and he didn't feel well.

He remembered bloody faces. From his dreams, and one from his most recent video. It was then he recalled what had happened last night, earlier that morning.

With an effort, he ripped his duvet away from his body. It had become tangled all over him, causing him to swelter. His rising anxiety wasn't helping that sweat to cease.

Simon could see the sun peeking through the blinds, but without his phone in the room he had no idea what time it was.

Whatever happened to clocks? he wondered vaguely as he lay back in bed, thinking more intently about what had happened before he'd fallen asleep.

Glitches. A series of glitches. Coincidences. That was all. This was his line of reasoning, and this was what gave him the strength to drag himself out of bed.

As he stood, he went from not feeling well to feeling outright awful. His skin felt hot, his stomach seemed to be loosely spinning about in his abdomen, unsettled. His head and heart drummed in tempo with one another. He felt his heart in his head and his headache all over his body, both pounding intensely.

He wondered briefly if it had been something he'd eaten. More likely it was a mix of several things he'd drunk. He didn't have a chance to think much more about the possibilities as he suddenly found that his mind was occupied with getting to the bathroom. Immediately. Moving at a sprint, he made his way to his toilet just in time to avoid throwing up all over the floor.

The sickness had been a necessary distraction, he would think later, because, after exiting the bathroom, he had gone immediately to his phone and, only once it was in his hand, did he remember the glitches. Though now, after a night of tumultuous tossing and turning, it was easier to tell himself that maybe he had dreamt some of what had occurred with his three devices.

The clock on his mobile device informed him that it was not yet noon, and the knowledge of how little sleep he'd gotten immediately drained him further.

Quickly replying to Jayne's good morning text, he let her know that he was sick.

The next thing he did, after feeling that unsettled turning of his stomach again, was send two additional text messages.

One was to his boss, telling him that he was ill, hadn't been able to sleep, and wouldn't be in tomorrow, Monday morning. Then he sent a similar text to his friend and co-worker, Martin. When one of them missed a day, the other picked up the slack. Simon hated to leave Martin hanging on a Monday, but included in the text that he would owe Martin several drinks and a bump.

Messages sent, he abandoned his phone again, went to the bathroom once more, then to his bed. And made that same back and forth trip repeatedly throughout the rest of his Sunday.

CHAPTER NINE

Simon felt better by midafternoon on Monday. Well enough to leave his bedroom, eat something solid, and turn on his television for the first time in over twenty-four hours, a record for him.

Picking up his phone, he saw that there were several messages and emails waiting for him. Ignoring the emails, he tended to the messages. The first was from his boss wishing him a speedy recovery. A few were from Jayne, who had greeted him with a her usual 'good morning', then, a few hours later, had sent a message inquiring if he was still alive.

He responded to her first, to put her mind at ease.

The next message he read gave him a genuine laugh after such a stressful night. It was from Martin.

You picked a hell of a day to play hooky bro. Melanie is wearing the shortest skirt I've ever seen outside of a nightclub. I just want to go in her office and let my face be her chair for the rest of the day. Get well soon.

To that, Simon responded:

You might want to be careful to avoid the stick up her ass.

The message left Simon with a smile on his face. The levity and normalcy of the exchange made him feel more at ease after the odd glitches he had been experiencing with the technology in his home, and the terror of the dreams he had woken up from on Sunday, nightmares which faded further as the days progressed.

The phone vibrated in his hand and Simon saw that Martin had sent him a photo. It was captioned:

Speaking of that ass.

The photo showed a poorly angled picture of a woman in a short skirt standing by the coffee machine in the employee kitchen where he and Martin worked. Looking at the photo, Simon almost wished he had gone to work to see that outfit on Melanie in person.

This was one of many candid photos that Martin had taken, not only of Melanie, but of several women who had worked with them over the years. Occasionally he took photos of customers as well. Simon took these same sorts of photographs from time to time, though with less frequency than his co-worker and friend. The two men were careful to only share these with each other. It made the monotony of Simon's daytime occupation more bearable.

He responded with:

Suddenly I'm feeling UP for COMING in today.

With that message he also sent a number of crude emojis that were intended to represent various fruits and vegetables. Martin's response was immediate:

LOL! Rest up. Hopefully I'll see you tomorrow.

The conversation, if you could call it that, made Simon feel better.

He checked his email and saw that one was from his connection at The Gore Report, Mr. Rood.

Over two million hits in one weekend. Great job, Simon. More videos like this and you can quit that day job of yours.

Simon beamed as he read this. He had asked his connection about permanent employment opportunities as a Gore Reporter. A contract that would make Simon's night work exclusive to this site. The Gore Report was his favourite of the taboo sites of its kind, and it paid him the most on average for his videos. But despite the fact that he had developed a good rapport with Mr. Rood, his connection always pushed back on the idea of taking him on as an employee. Now it seemed it could be a possibility. Simon, in his jubilation, was about to click the link that was sent along with the email. The link to the video. He wanted to see the hits, to read the comments. Then, remembering the glitches more vividly, he decided not to indulge in any of the above.

He responded politely, humbly, and with a promise that he would do his best to provide Mr. Rood with more quality content. Simon was certain that if he produced one more valuable video, he could send it to Rood in exchange for the contract he hoped for rather than just a lump sum. He wanted more than ever to be rid of his day job. As much as he liked Martin and his boss, reporting the truth about society was where his heart lay. But, for now, he felt like he was due a bit of time off from both jobs.

Resisting the urge to check on the success of his latest work, Simon instead put down his phone, went back to his room, and spent the rest of the day reading his slightly sweat-stained book.

CHAPTER TEN

The rest of Simon's Monday off went well and, by the end of it, he had not only finished reading *1984* but had also convinced himself that the strangeness of the Sunday morning had just been a combination of the excitement, the drugs, the booze and a series of technological malfunctions.

By Tuesday morning he had put the ordeal almost entirely behind him.

Arriving a few minutes late for work as he typically did, Simon got out of his car and walked into the dealership that was his place of employment.

After an impromptu day off, the well-liked car salesman had expected a warm greeting from the people he had grown to think of as his work family. But it didn't take Simon long to understand that something was wrong.

Each person he encountered looked at him oddly, many of them averting their eyes and not saying hello, even when he addressed them directly. Others frowned at him, glaring outright. The receptionist – sweet seventy-year-old Mrs. Patterson who had been there since the decades-old building had first been opened as a brand-new creation – had let Simon know he was needed in Mr. Chase's office immediately. When Simon asked her what the issue was, the white-haired woman simply presented to him her middle finger and glared directly into his eyes, into his soul, before she went back to her work, a phone call interrupting their interaction.

Simon was befuddled. He remained that way as he walked anxiously through the showroom filled with shining, brand-new vehicles and entered the office of Cody Chase, manager of this establishment.

His confusion only increased when he saw Martin in the office, sitting across from Mr. Chase, the manager's large black glass desk between them. Both men looked at Simon with concern as he entered the office.

"What's going on?" Simon asked, his voice shakier than he would have liked it to sound. Though the discomfort over his shaky voice didn't last long as Simon nearly had to lunge back out of the room with the way Martin reacted to his question.

"You gonna fucking pretend you don't know what you did?" Martin said, and, to Simon, it looked as though his friend and co-worker of half a decade was struggling to restrain himself. Like he was having a hard time not jumping out of his seat and punching Simon square in the jaw. Martin spat out,

"I'm surprised you even showed up today." Then he turned away from Simon, looking instead in the direction of Mr. Chase's prized memorabilia wall – a shrine to athleticism full of sports mementos, autographed baseball bats and signed balls of all variety from the many sports teams of the Toronto area, the metropolis which neighboured Saturn City.

"What the fuck is happening right now? Mrs. Patterson just gave me the finger and you two are acting like a pair of assholes. What is it that everyone thinks I did?" Simon said at a distressed decibel. Both Martin and Mr. Chase looked at each other quizzically.

Typically, an employee who seemed to be in a bit of trouble wouldn't address his employer in such a manner. But Mr. Chase was practically Simon and Martin's older brother. When he had been selected to manage this dealership, they were among his first hires. Two young college graduates who were eager for work of any sort,

Simon and Martin had grown together in this business with the guidance of their boss over the last five years. To Simon, Cody Chase was almost as much a friend as Martin was.

Chase reached for his mobile device, which was on the desk in front of him. His large fingers slid, pressed, clicked. He raised the device – screen first – to Simon.

"You mean to tell me you don't remember sending these text messages to every single person who works here?" Chase asked, genuinely sounding confused, also sounding slightly suspicious.

Simon leaned over the desk, looked at the screen. It didn't take long for his face to twist into surprise, shock, awe, disbelief.

On the screen in front of him were sentences such as:

I just want to go in her office and let my face be her chair for the rest of the day.

Messages stating:

Christ, have you seen Melanie's pants today? It's Clam O'clock again.

Responses like:

You mean camel toe'clock. Fuck, I wish I was her pants.

There was a string of these, mostly about Melanie, though there were comments about other women from the office as well. Simon couldn't believe his eyes. He turned to Martin, furious.

"What the fuck? Why would you put this out there?"

"Why would *I*?" Martin rose from his chair, nearly knocking it over in his haste. If Chase hadn't risen up as well, signalling for Martin to be calm from across the large, cluttered desk which separated them, there may have been bloodshed in the office on this day.

Martin struggled to maintain the calm that Chase had asked for, managing to restrain himself despite his anger. To recapture his composure enough to say,

"Those messages show as coming from *your* phone, you dumb fuck. Now because of you my career is over."

"What?" Simon asked. Disbelief occupied most of his mind, worry took up the rest. He reached into his pocket for his phone. And, just as he was about to punch in his password, an unfamiliar anxiousness gripped him. He was worried about what he would see when the screen cleared and gave him access to the files on his mobile device. He ignored the feeling. Punched in his code. Checked his sent messages, and nearly dropped the phone in abject shock.

"Hacked..." Simon said. He repeated, "I must have been hacked. I didn't send these..."

Yet he saw that they had been sent from his device. Message after forwarded message sent to his co-workers and boss. Several of the salacious and perverted thoughts that had been shared between he and Martin. Photos of Melanie's ass in several candid situations. Simon went to say more, to defend himself, but he was at a loss for words as he scrolled through the messages. Texts displaying Simon's lost future in the form of crude comments concerning cunts and cunnilingus.

"My God... We're fucked." was all he managed to squeak out. Again, Martin gave him a look that reminded Simon of a soon to be uncoiled snake, ready to strike. Fortunately for Simon, Chase once again cooled things.

"No one's fucked." Chase stated calmly, though with irritation as the undertone to that calm. "I run this place, and you boys have helped me build it up to what it is today. Far as I'm concerned, you haven't done anything wrong. Other than being a pair of sloppy idiots."

"Chase... I swear, I was hack—"

"Quit the shit, Simon. I don't give a fuck if you were hacked. You were *sloppy*! Don't you think I've looked at Melanie and thought to myself I'd like to put my tongue so far up that tight little asshole that we wind up French kissing? Of course I have! The only thing is I won't fucking text about it. Because 'that's not appropriate'." He said that last sentence mockingly. Then chuckled before he continued, "I need you to understand that there will be a lot of pressure on me to fire you two if Melanie makes any real noise about this. She's pissed, but she's not one of the vengeful ones, fortunately.

"Luckily for you, she came to me this morning and not directly to head office. We managed to work out a solution. What I'm going to do is suspend you both for a week. We'll set you up with an online sexual harassment sensitivity training course during your suspension." When he saw the looks of concern on their faces, Chase added, with a grin, "Don't worry, it's only a two-hour thing. And it'll put the people here at ease. The fact that you didn't actually *say* anything sexual to her is what's helping your case the most. But, honest to God, pictures and texts? You guys are younger than I am, you should know better. Women these days can't even take a joke or a compliment. We don't need to give them any more ammo than what they're already drumming up in their pretty little heads."

Neither Simon nor Martin said anything. Both still stewing. Chase continued,

"Get your apologies ready. Melanie is waiting outside in her car. I talked her out of getting an advocate, and she agreed to stay on if you guys agree to get help." Chase chuckled after this. He got up and walked toward the door as he said, "When she comes in here, you grovel. Your phone was hacked. This situation has now shown you the error of your ways, and you two are changed men hoping to be even more changed once you graduate from your training course." He paused with his hand on the doorknob, turned back toward Simon and Martin, looked both men directly in their eyes, then, right before walking out, said, "Seriously though, I don't need this shit. This better be the last time. Simon, update your phone's security. You're too smart to be this stupid." Then he walked out of the room, and Simon was forced to confront the ice-cold stare of one of his closest friends.

"Martin. Listen."

Martin didn't listen, he interrupted instead.

"Delete the pictures. And the texts. Right now."

"What?" Simon asked.

"Your fucking phone." Martin clarified, and the fact that he had to explain this filled the man with an unholy rage, though he somehow maintained his calm. "Take out your phone and delete everything we've ever sent to each other. They haven't seen all of it. I would hate for you to get 'hacked' again." Martin said, then said no more. Only glared at Simon as Simon went to do what Martin had demanded.

Frustrated and confused, Simon uttered a series of curses as he looked down at his phone. It seemed to be glitching again. This time the voice recorder app was on. His phone had somehow been recording.

"What? What's going on?" Martin asked, a great deal of concern in his voice. Simon ignored him, was busy trying to figure out why his phone had been operating seemingly on its own. He went to hit stop, and nearly dropped the device entirely when it stopped recording on its own before his thumb could touch it.

"Simon. What is going on?" Martin asked again, this time with panic in his voice. Simon was about to look up at Martin and explain to him that his phone was acting strangely, hoped that showing him this new evidence of such would prove that it was the phone's fault more so than his, but at that moment the voice recorder program on the device stopped recording and began to play. At least it looked like it was playing. No sound came out of the phone itself.

"Honestly, Martin, I have no cl–"

He heard a sound over the building's loudspeakers. A bubbling sound, a choking gurgle, like someone trying to clear a throat quickly filling with liquid. To Martin he said,

"Do you hear that?"

"Hear what?" Martin had gotten up and was standing by the vertical blinds covering the office window that Chase often looked out of when sitting at his desk. He was peeking out and looking at the showroom floor.

"You better have that shit deleted." Martin said, the panic in his voice turning to menace. "And figure out what you're going to say to Melanie. She and Chase are on their way back right no–"

A different sound projecting from the building's speakers stopped him cold. And this time there was no doubt that he could hear it just as well as Simon could. It was no longer the gurgling sound of a dying man. It was a voice, a familiar one.

Over the loudspeaker came the voice of Cody Chase, which should have been impossible because Chase was nowhere near a device that would have been able to project his words. Still, his voice was playing over the Public Announcement system:

"You were sloppy! Don't you think I've looked at Melanie and thought to myself I'd like to put my tongue so far up that tight little asshole that we wind up French kissing? Of course I have! The only thing is I won't fucking text about it. Because 'that's not appropriate'." The mockery was clear in his voice as it played over the speakers throughout the building, clearer still was the laughter which followed that mocking statement.

The voice of Chase skipped. Started again:

"Women these days can't even take a joke or a compliment. We don't need to give them any more ammo than what they're already drumming up in their pretty little heads."

It skipped again. Started once more:

"Don't you think I've looked at Melanie and thought to myself I'd like to put my tongue so far up that tight little asshole that we wind up French kissing?"

It stopped. Repeated:

"That tight little asshole... That tight little asshole..."

The recorded voice of Cody Chase continued to be replayed for everyone in the building to hear.

It didn't take Simon long to realize that it was his phone somehow playing this over the speakers. He tried to stop it several times, but it only continued to roll. Repeating snippets or whole sentences of what Cody Chase had just been telling them in private. Simon got up from his seat, joined Martin by the windows, sweat gathering on his brow, his lip, several other places including the palms with which he reached clammily toward the blinds, aiming to pull them aside and see if maybe by some chance the recording had only played in this one room and not everywhere for everyone to hear. But the moment he pulled back the blinds he saw commotion.

Cody Chase was practically surrounded by half a dozen of his female employees, some of them looking shellshocked, others gesticulating wildly at the speakers, at Mr. Chase, at each other. The dealership wasn't officially open for the day, and Simon was thankful no customers were there to give strength to this potential lynching.

Chase had his hands up and in front of him as though he had a weapon aimed at his chest, as though he expected to be struck. He looked from the crowd of women near him to the one woman who was leaving the area.

Melanie was running through the showroom, out of the building. Simon could see her from his vantage in Chase's office. And, for the first time he could remember, he didn't take the opportunity to check out her ass as she exited a room.

"Jesus Christ..." Martin said, then his voice trailed off as Chase's voice over the speakers overwhelmed it. Still repeating crudities throughout the store.

Simon was speechless. He kept trying to stop his phone from playing, to power it down, but it wouldn't respond. Only continued to play the recording.

Simon looked up from his phone just in time to see tiny, old Mrs. Patterson walk right up to Cody Chase and slap him across the mouth.

It was at this point that the recording of Chase finally stopped playing over the speaker system. It was also at this point that Chase stopped speaking to the employees who surrounded him. Stopped trying to defend himself. Instead, he turned and looked toward his office, seemed to make direct eye contact with Simon who was looking through the blinds at the scene on the showroom floor. Simon recoiled and stepped away from the window as Chase pointed at him, then began to storm back toward the office. The man had never looked so angry in all the years Simon had known him.

"We're fucked." Simon muttered. It didn't take long for Martin to respond.

"No, dickhead. *You're* fucked."

Martin was correct about that, because when Cody Chase – Simon's boss and long-time friend – burst into the room and looked at the two men, both of his eyes the colour of pure rage, Martin immediately pointed at Simon. Said,

"It wasn't any kind of hack, Chase. This snitching fuck was setting us up the whole time. He's the one who recorded you!"

That was all it took for Chase to turn on one of his longest tenured employees.

'No!" Simon protested. "Chase, listen, my phone has been acting crazy lately! Cody, God damnit, you have to believe me!"

Ignoring these feeble protests, Chase made his way over to Simon, his body driven by wordless fury.

Chase grabbed two fistfuls of what was no longer a well-pressed shirt. A shirt no longer as dry as it had been minutes ago. Simon had been sweating profusely since the recording had begun playing over the speakers. Now – his forehead, his armpits, his back, his balls – he was producing waterfalls all over his body.

"Cody. Listen to m–"

When Simon had started this sentence, Chase had begun to clear his throat. He, being a smoker, constantly had a buildup of phlegm at the back of his mouth. When Simon had stopped talking, he had done so because that phlegm, along with a copious amount of saliva, had been gathered into Cody's mouth and subsequently released.

The loogey landed mostly on Simon's nose and cheek, though, because he had been speaking as he was spat upon, some of Chase's spittle made its way into his mouth.

He retched, spat on the floor, wiped at his face furiously with his shirt sleeve, only further smearing the phlegmy saliva into his skin.

Doing his best not to throw up, trying his hardest to not lash out, Simon intended to reason with the two men in the room, but, before he had even made a sound, Chase looked at Simon with eyes that sprayed shrapnel. If the look wasn't cutting enough, the words Chase said were.

"You're done here, you pathetic little pussy. But don't think for a second that I'm done with you."

Simon swallowed his pride (along with, he thought, a bit of Chase's spit) and walked out of the room without begging any further. Every eye on the showroom floor was on him. He avoided those gazes, ignored the people who were calling out to him as he made his way to the exit of the building at a pace that was nearly a sprint, believing in his heart that he would never see this place or these people again. Believing that his career, his reputation, perhaps even his future, were over.

CHAPTER ELEVEN

"I can go and cut him if that's what you want. You can even film it. It'll make us some money and the world will be a better place. Two birds, one knife." Jayne said to Simon through the phone. She was speaking about Cody Chase.

Simon laughed at this on a day he had believed all laughter would be extinguished.

His phone had gone off frequently after he had rushed out of the dealership earlier that day. He had been hesitant to even look at the thing, no longer trusting what had been his favourite piece of technology. But after several hours had gone by with Simon sitting in his living room watching daytime television, attempting to drink away the day, a string of nearly nonstop message alerts and missed phone calls made it so he finally couldn't help but check his device.

What he saw had astounded him. There was a plethora of messages and missed calls from many of the women he worked with. That wasn't a surprise. What surprised him was the fact that these messages were not the hateful, scornful sort he had expected. These were messages of consolation. Messages of concern. Texts to say 'thank you'.

He couldn't believe his eyes. He decided to confirm with his ears, checking his voicemail to hear, with growing disbelief, the voice of Mrs. Patterson, not only apologizing for giving him the finger that morning, but thanking him for being a hero and standing up for the women he worked with.

There was a string of voicemail similar to Mrs. Patterson's. Including one that nearly made Simon's heart turn to rolling thunder in his chest.

It was from head office. One of the many higher ups that Simon had only seen from a distance at holiday parties or conferences.

It turned out, according to this representative, that Chase had been incorrect about Simon being done at the dealership. Instead, Chase had been fired within hours once word had reached head office of that morning's events. That word included someone's recording of the recording of Chase which had played over the speakers. His termination was unavoidable.

Simon was told that someone from head office would be at the dealership the following morning to sort things out until a new and appropriate manager could be selected. In the meanwhile, Simon was asked to call back and speak about the situation. There was also an offer to take the rest of the week off. Paid. A bit of a mental health break, a vacation for his troubles and his heroics.

Heroics! Simon was giddy at the thought of that, had nearly danced after listening to this message, not knowing that he could go from rock bottom to sky high in a matter of moments.

He felt guilty about Chase, and he imagined Martin wouldn't be far behind their boss on the unemployment line, but the feelings of guilt fled quickly as he remembered Martin pointing at him, blaming him without even giving him the benefit of the doubt. The feelings of guilt were gone entirely when he remembered the ashy, sour taste of Chase's spittle in his mouth, the feeling of his boss's mucus sliding down his face. No, Simon told himself, he had nothing to feel guilty about. His phone had malfunctioned.

He couldn't be blamed for that. Besides, no one had forced Chase to say the things he'd said.

After receiving the unexpected good news, he temporarily forgot about the trouble with his phone, scrolling through his messages and responding when responding was necessary, calling back when he had to, eventually calling Jayne and letting her know a version of what had happened at work. Which is what he was doing now.

"No need to cut him, J." Simon told her, responding to his girlfriend's joke. "I think he's done enough damage to himself as it is."

"You sound like you feel sorry for him."

"Well... he hired me. And he's always been kind to me. I just had no idea how much of a dirtbag he was." Simon lied. He, Martin and Chase had gone out together many times outside of work hours. Together the three had explored strip clubs, seedy massage parlours, hotel rooms brimming with cocaine and hookers. He knew exactly what Mr. Chase was. The two were cut from the same cloth.

"His wife is going to kill him. I can't take any pleasure in a man potentially losing his family."

"But he tried to blame you..."

"He did. I'm sure Martin got some of the blame as well. He was the one who brought up Melanie's outfit from yesterday before Chase just went off on this tirade about everything he wanted to do to her. It was gross. And she was right there at the doorway listening to it all. I saw her, but I was so surprised that I didn't say anything right away. I basically let the man hang himself, and I don't feel great about it."

It was a flimsy story he had told Jayne. A flimsy story full of holes. But Jayne trusted Simon completely. Didn't try to fill those holes with logic. He said it, she believed it. That's generally how things went with them. That was a large part of why he loved her.

The thing about people, Simon had learned a long time ago, is that if you tell them a secret dark enough – something they believe to be your darkest secret – they tend to trust that you will not keep any other secrets from them. That you are not capable of making more.

Simon thought of his secrets. Thought of milk. Knew there were things that Jayne could never understand.

"Well, you have nothing to feel bad about. Chase said what he said. You didn't make him say disgusting things out loud within earshot of his female employees. What a dick."

"Yeah, well, after everyone saw him lose his shit on me and some of the others, head office gave a few of us the rest of the week off. Paid. So it wasn't all bad." Another partial truth. One thing he would never include in this version of events was the spit. Would likely never repeat that detail for the rest of his days.

"Lucky you. If I didn't have to wake up at the ass crack of dawn every day this week, I would suggest we celebrate this little vacation of yours."

"Oh, we will." he said. "After the party on Saturday, we'll celebrate plenty."

"Promise?" Her voice was eager anticipation.

"Pinky swear." was his response.

The conversation ended soon after that. Simon was smiling when he got off the phone. Grinning until he put the device down on the couch beside him, looked at it, and remembered that it was the source of so many of his recent issues. He recalled Martin's advice from earlier in the day, about deleting everything – text messages, photos, videos, all of it. And that is exactly what he spent the next little while doing.

CHAPTER TWELVE

Simon felt better about his situation as the day went on. His phone was cleared, his important videos and documents all backed up on his laptop. Whatever was causing the glitches – and he refused to believe it was anything other than a series of malfunctions – seemed to have ceased. He was able to relax and watch a string of lighthearted comedy movies to get his mind off the strangeness of his last few days.

He drank whiskey as he watched what he watched, and eventually fell asleep on his couch not long after midnight.

Less than an hour after drifting off, Simon was roused by a knocking on his door.

He thought, briefly, that he was dreaming. Ignored the knock. Then the knock became a banging. Not repeated but methodical. Like someone taking their time to wind up before they laid their hand to the door each time.

Bang. Pause. **Bang.** Pause. **Bang.**

Simon was wide awake now. He reached for his phone just in case he had to call the police, but saw that his phone was off. Tried to turn it on but it wouldn't respond. Simon looked at a black and blank screen, one which somehow projected dismal portents.

Bang. Pause. **Bang.** Pause. **Bang.**

Simon didn't know what to do. Was going to call out to see who was there. Before he could open his mouth to do so, the person at the door seemed to lose the little bit of restraint they possessed.

Bang Bang Bang Bang Bang Bang Bang!

"Open the fucking door you snitching little bitch!"

It was Chase. Simon recognized the voice immediately.

Fuck, is what Simon thought as he twisted around on the couch, looking at his front door from his living room. With a great deal of resolve he stood up, walked toward the door.

"Chase?" he said hesitantly. "Dude, it was a misunderstand—"

One loud crash.

Simon witnessed in disbelief his door being kicked in, splinters flying from the frame as it ruptured from the force of Chase's big boot.

All at once Cody Chase was inside of Simon's apartment, reeking of booze and ash and ill intentions. In one of his hands he carried a baseball bat. Simon saw signatures scribbled all over it and recognized the bat as one of the many pieces of memorabilia that had been hanging on Chase's office wall just earlier that day.

"Whoa! Chase. You need to calm down. What happened earlier was an accident. I've tried to explain that. My phone has been acting crazy all week."

Chase, who had been stomping further into the apartment, suddenly stopped. The fury on his face dropped, shock overtook his countenance. Then, to Simon's surprise (and concern), Chase began to laugh.

It was not a friendly sound.

Chase reached into his pocket. Simon, for a terrible moment, expected his former boss and friend to pull out a gun, but instead he produced a cell phone. The fury returned to his face as he waved his phone wildly at Simon as though it was a pistol.

"Was it your fucked up phone that's been texting me all night and gloating about me losing my job? Huh? Telling me that I got what I deserve. Was it an accident when you typed out that you hope my fucking wife *leaves* me!" His voice cracked at this last bit. His face twisted, and Simon believed Chase was going to cry. Witnessing this would have been a first for Simon. Never had he seen the alpha male come anywhere close to being this overcome with emotion. He was hoping for tears at this point, wanting to console and calm Chase.

He never got the chance.

The rage had once again replaced whatever emotion had almost gripped Chase. He shoved his phone back in his pocket, placed both hands on the bat, and started swinging and screaming simultaneously.

"You want to destroy my life?" The bat smashed against the full-length mirror of the closet near the entrance. Shattered glass soon covered the floor. Chase crunched over it as he proceeded to slowly pursue Simon, seeming to enjoy the fear he was seeing on Simon's face.

"Think you can set me up and *laugh* about it?"

The bat made a hole in the wall, then another. A third.

Simon was backing into his living room now. He had backed into his couch, and was trying to shuffle sideways around it, hoping to get to the other side of the couch and put some space between him and Chase, who was busy putting more holes in the wall.

Chase marauded through the hallway causing damage with each step, until he was clear of the front hall and no longer looked interested in putting holes in Simon's walls.

Warm up hacks, Simon thought as Chase's eyes locked onto his own. The practice swings were over, Chase now had his sights set squarely on Simon's head.

"Listen. Chase. I was *hacked*! I swear! My phone isn't even on!"

At that moment, from behind him on the couch, Simon's mobile device began to ring, sounding like an old-fashioned landline telephone. It wasn't a ringtone he had ever heard come from his device.

He paused.

Chase paused.

The phone was like alarm bells sounding off, proving Simon a liar in Chase's eyes. Confirming every ill thought he'd had as he'd made his way across town, drunk and high, on this revenge mission.

Simon understood that the time for words was over.

Chase raised the bat over his head, swung down as though he was a man hard at work chopping firewood just as Simon decided to sprint instead of shuffle. The bat came down on the back of the couch where Simon had been standing. Something in the chair cracked. Simon was grateful it hadn't been his skull.

He ran into his living room hoping to make it to his kitchen and grab something he could defend himself with.

He didn't make it there.

As he neared the kitchen he was tackled from behind and rudely introduced to his unforgiving floor. He landed mostly on his shoulder but managed to hit his head as well, hard enough to daze him but not knock him unconscious.

Chase was shifting his considerable weight on top of Simon. Mounting him. Simon managed to squirm his body in such a way that he hoped he would be able to push his assailant off of him, maybe reach up and gouge at his eyes. Anything to stop Chase from continuing this attack.

The moment he managed to get onto his back, however, Chase had taken the bat and lain it across Simon's neck. His left hand on the barrel, his right clutching the handle, Chase proceeded to press down with no relent, no intention of mercy. Simon went from hoping he could defend himself to simply hoping to survive. He did his best to push up on the baseball bat as it threatened to crush his throat, to stop his air and seize his life.

The two men grunted as they battled against each other. The sounds of attempted murder and desperate survival were the only ones that filled the room, other than that of Simon's phone which had never stopped braying its alarm-like ring.

It was the last thing Simon thought he would ever hear, that taunting ring. Being smaller, weaker, and not aided by gravity as Chase was at the moment, or driven by the rage which had possessed his former boss, Simon began to fade under the pressure of the bat across his neck.

"Chase. Please." he tried to say, but it came out as a pair of hisses. Wasted wind. Though with the sound came a change in Chase's face. Something in his eyes brightened. He let up on the bat, stopped pressing down so thoroughly. Allowed Simon to gasp for air, cough, feel relief. Momentarily.

Simon saw that the man was raising the bat, still with each hand gripping the barrel and handle. He realized that Chase was about to bring the middle of the bat down onto his forehead, bashing it in. He couldn't believe it. Couldn't believe it had come to this.

"Please," he tried to say. A wheeze. Barely audible air.

"My wife is gone, Simon. She took my little girls with her. Because of you! And you *laughed*. Not so fucking funny now, huh? You're not such a tough guy now, are you?"

Then he went to bring the bat down, delighted malice in his eyes. Simon, too weak from his strangling to do anything in terms of a defence, closed his eyes and waited for the pain.

There was a thud. A whacking sound. Wood on bone.

Simon felt no pain in that moment. Felt no pain because he hadn't been hit.

He opened his eyes just in time to see Chase's body slide off him, collapsing to the ground, the bat falling with him, clanking then rolling along the floor until it came to a stop against the wall. Confused, Simon looked up to see a neighbour of his standing over both he and a now unconscious Chase whose limp legs were still atop him.

Simon scurried away from Chase and, with a great deal of effort, managed to rise to a sitting position, hugging his knees with his arms as he attempted to process what was going on.

At that moment the phone stopped ringing, and Simon was nearly as grateful for that as he was to see his neighbour, standing there wielding a baseball bat of his own. The sound of the phone had been threatening to drive him mad. Though, with the events of the last few days, he wondered if he hadn't arrived at lunacy already.

Simon didn't know the name of the man who had saved him, but they were cordial when they encountered each other in the halls or the elevator. And, just as they did on most occasions in the hallway, they nodded at one another.

"Thank you," Simon managed to wheeze out, rubbing his tender neck while still trying to gather his wind. He heard the sound of approaching feet and murmured noise. Looking past his neighbour at his open front door, he noticed a few other neighbours in the hallway. Some were dressed in robes and pajamas, some dressed in far too little. All were peeking into his unit to see what the commotion had been about now that it had gone silent. A few of them had their phones out, ready to document the aftermath of the event that had roused them. Witnesses, not heroes.

Looking at the man who had saved him, Simon had never been more grateful in his life. Became even more so when the man went to the door and closed it on the prying eyes. Tried to lock it and, seeing that the frame was shattered, leaned his bulk against the door instead.

"Goddamn vultures. Everyone is a paparazzo now," he said in a South Asian accent threaded with exasperation. Simon only nodded in agreement. Hoping that none of them had captured anything worth posting.

He went over the entire interaction between himself and Chase, pictured it from the perspective of someone filming. Knew it was a money maker, an immediate viral sensation. He was fortunate no one had caught it.

"Now." Simon's neighbour continued. "Would you care to tell me just what is going on here?"

CHAPTER THIRTEEN

It turned out that his neighbour's name was Abdul. Simon heard the name for the first time when the police came knocking on his door, asking both men to identify themselves. Then asking what had happened. The officers had arrived at his unit only a minute or two after Abdul had. They would have been a minute too late had he not been there first.

Simon had presented to the police and Abdul a version of what had happened, followed by an insistence that Chase not be jailed but hospitalized instead.

"He's under a lot of stress... Just lost his job... Mental health issues... An isolated episode... Regularly contributes to charities... Just lost his family... Needs to get help, not be put behind bars..." Simon yammered on, desperately defending the man who had nearly taken his life. The defence was the result of some of that same guilt he believed had fled him earlier in the day, now returned full on. He was angry, of course, but he understood. It hadn't been Chase's fault. It had been whatever had corrupted Simon's phone.

Simon had quickly glanced at his phone just before the police arrived, and what he saw there had astounded him. That was what truly brought the guilt back, driving it deep. He knew he would continue to defend Chase throughout whatever would come next. He had to.

A hacker, he continued to tell himself. *It has to be a hacker.*

After the ambulance had come to take a still unconscious Chase away, and after the police and medics and Abdul had said goodbye, leaving Simon to himself, he went to check his phone. To confirm what he had seen before. To take a look at it more thoroughly.

When Chase had originally barged through the door, rambling about their supposed exchange of messages, Simon believed that Chase had likely taken a few bumps of coke and several drinks too many. But, after seeing what was waiting for him on his phone, Simon wondered if it was he who might be high, drunk. Losing his mind.

There were dozens of messages between him and Chase, even though he had deleted all of his text messages earlier that evening before falling asleep.

Frantically, heart pounding, confused, he scrolled up to the first message. Saw what he had been terrified of seeing. The string of conversation had begun that evening, and, to his growing dismay, had been started by Simon. Or at least whoever was hacking Simon's phone.

You're lucky I didn't knock you out for spitting on me. You deserve everything that's coming to you.

That message had been ignored. Simon's phone had sent another.

Try something like that again and see what happens.

No response. Again. Then again. At least ten messages had been sent by Simon's phone, each of them had been ignored before Chase had finally snapped after reading:

Your wife and kids deserve better than you.

He had responded then, answering with several expletives and detailed threats. Chase and Simon's hacker had gone back and forth, the rage and toxicity and danger of the interaction increasing with each message.

Finally, there was the final message from Simon's phone, one that Simon had trouble comprehending. It read:

OK tough guy. You know where I live. Buzzer number 4625 just in case you forgot. But you don't have the balls just like you don't have a job or a family. Prove me wrong, bitch.

This was followed by several emojis intended to portray laughter and joy, used as mockery here.

After reading through the texts, Simon wasn't shocked that Chase had shown up in the state he had been in roughly an hour after that last message had been sent. Simon felt confident in his decision to not have Chase taken to jail. Psychiatric help was exactly what the man required. Messages like those sent from Simon's phone would drive anybody mad.

"A hacker." he whispered to himself, his voice devoid of confidence. "It _has_ to be."

Simon went to delete the string of messages, but before his finger could touch the screen, one by one, they began to be deleted on their own. To disappear, to vanish. Like a ghost.

"No, no, no, no. It's a hacker. It has to be." he said to himself, trying to pump veracity into his voice, hoping that he would believe it if it sounded convincing to his own ears. But he was having a hard time being convinced.

For the second time that week, Simon kept all the lights in his apartment on, this time laying on his couch instead of his bed because of his broken front door. He waited for daylight, another book in hand, a butcher knife within reach on the coffee table. He was well aware that sleep would not arrive for him that night.

CHAPTER FOURTEEN

Shortly after daylight broke on Wednesday morning, Simon was contacted by a member of the building's maintenance staff. He had left a message for the manager of the building after the police had gone, informing him of the holes in his walls and the broken door and broken mirror in his apartment. Simon was promised that his doorjamb and frame would be fixed by day's end.

A maintenance man was there by noon and gone not long after fixing the door and filling and patching up the holes in Simon's walls. The shattered mirror would have to wait, however. Simon had long since swept up the shards, wondering if Chase's seven years of bad luck for this act would somehow be shared with him.

He was left with a new reinforced lock in place of the old one. And an improved feeling about his physical security. Simon also felt better about his cyber security at this point, having spent a portion of the night stripping his phone, clearing it, removing every app, restoring it to its factory setting and installing a virus protection program that assured he would be hacker free. Because, he repeatedly told himself, it *had* to be a hacker. The alternative was too crazy to give credence too.

Still, Simon was careful.

He deactivated then deleted his social media, which was no big loss to him. He only had a Facebook account. One which he infrequently checked. A waste of space on his phone, really, he told himself.

He wasn't fond of social media. Too many counterfeit and toxic people trying desperately to spread their falsities and toxicity to the world one heavily edited photo, ill-thought out post or crude comment at a time. The poisonousness of mainstream social media was catching. Fast spreading. And Simon had always been eager to avoid it.

At least on the gore sites people were themselves. They didn't pretend. They knew what they were there for and were real about it. That was what Simon respected. That was part of the reason he did what he did. Or, why he did what he decided he would now be taking a break from.

Although he had the week off, he had no intention of using that time to scour the neighbourhoods. Wasn't motivated to find another victim of their own circumstances. Couldn't imagine making another video just then. It had been a long and trying week, and it was only Wednesday afternoon. The last few days had left him feeling unsettled. Out of sorts. He was worried, he was anxious. Those were two words he rarely used in association with himself. However, the first half of this week had been like none he had ever experienced. Several days that felt more like a year. Now he had the rest of the week off, and all Simon wanted to do during this brief vacation was to relax. To disconnect.

He did just that.

Eventually.

There were issues he couldn't entirely avoid at first, unfortunately for him. Issues such as the situation concerning his former boss.

Late Wednesday afternoon Simon was contacted by first the police and then Cody Chase's lawyer.

There would be a court date, Simon was informed. Chase had been charged even though he had been hospitalized and not jailed. The charges were unlawful entry and assault. Simon – and Abdul at Simon's insistence

– had downplayed how bad the attack was. How close to death Simon had been.

Simon was told that Chase's charges would likely be suspended when all was said and done. His former boss and friend would be given, by the courts, something called a Mental Health Diversion. It would be a chance for Chase to get a fresh start, his lawyer – a woman who sounded aged, nasal and hurried – let Simon know. She inquired, based on the police report, if Simon would agree to testify on Chase's behalf. He agreed without hesitation, eager to end the call and put his phone away.

He spent the rest of Wednesday watching eighties comedy movies and eating food he knew wasn't good for him.

On Thursday, Jayne came over to spend the night. Due to her hectic schedule, it was a rare occurrence that she would sleep over during the week. Though, because he had nowhere to be in the morning, he didn't mind that she would have to wake up – and subsequently wake him up – at 5 AM to scurry out of his apartment.

The lovers took full advantage of their impromptu night together. But first, there was some awkwardness.

"He broke in your door? He was *that* mad at you?" Jayne asked. She had noticed the reinforced lock and missing mirror immediately. Simon had been planning on telling her what had happened (a slightly altered version of events) when they had settled down for the evening, but it wound up being the first thing they talked about after she had entered his home. He'd promised her repeatedly that he wasn't in danger.

With both of them on the couch, their bodies turned toward each other, him holding her hand, her with eyes made of concern and dismay. He explained,

"Something's gone wrong in his head, Jayne. I've never seen him look so confused. He said that his wife left him after hearing about what type of guy he is from some of the ladies at work. She took his daughters too. I guess he kinda just lost it and needed someone to unload on. He wasn't himself and I don't blame him."

She sucked in air, the sound was a hiss of disapproval.

"You don't blame a guy who blamed *you* for his own shit, broke your door down, smashed your mirror and punched a bunch of holes in your wall?"

Simon hadn't mentioned the baseball bat. Hadn't mentioned being tackled, straddled, nearly killed. Jayne believed that Cody Chase had broken into the house to throw a very intense temper tantrum, and that the neighbours had called the police to take him away after several minutes of his rages.

"I can't blame him. It's a mental health thing. The guy's been doing coke and worse since he was a teenager. High pressure job, just got exposed as a sleaze, *and* his wife and family ditched him? Any of that could have been the straw that broke the camel's back. How would I look if I decided to start kicking a crippled camel while he was down?"

"You know," Jayne said, after a brief pause and a slowly spreading smile, "I sometimes forget how wise you are."

Simon, knowing what that smile meant (other than her believing his half-truth entirely), said,

"Anything else you might have forgotten since the last time we were alone together?"

For a time after that they were done with words – sighs, grunts, moans replaced them.

Jayne had missed Simon, had been worried about him. This was clear from how she ravaged him. He, too, missed her. Missed this bit of normalcy after the week he'd had, and he clung to the return of that normalcy desperately. For the first time in months, Simon focused only on Jayne.

He didn't have to resort to the mental reel of porn and past pleasures he usually had to go to when he needed to find his climax. He didn't think of his mistress, who he had been actively putting out of his mind knowing he wouldn't be able to be with her any time soon. For the first time in a long time, it was only he and Jayne in his head, in his bed. And Simon was grateful for every moment with her.

That night he slept peacefully, without worrying about his phone, for the first time in nearly a week.

CHAPTER FIFTEEN

When Jayne had gone to work, while the sun was still preparing to make its appearance on that Friday morning, she left behind the piece of normalcy she had brought with her the night before. Simon enjoyed this gift as much as any he had ever received. So relaxed was Simon that he was able to go back to bed after she had left, and slept until it was midafternoon, catching up on the hours of slumber which had eluded him so far that week.

He nearly felt like a new man when he woke up, a new man with an old familiar itch. By evening time, Simon was considering going on the hunt for new material, prowling around the clubs and shady neighbourhoods in downtown Saturn until he found something that might fetch him a pretty penny, and put him in even better standing with the owner of The Gore Report. He considered this but concluded that it might be a bad idea. Something like tempting fate. He had escaped enough danger for one week, Simon reminded himself. He didn't want to push his luck. So, while he wouldn't allow himself to go out to prowl, he decided to log onto thegorereport.com. He wanted to see what had been uploaded since his video had been posted. And he wanted to see if any of it compared to his recording, though he wasn't in a rush to see the video itself.

There had been a handful of new clips and several still images posted in the last week. He saw nothing spectacular. Standard fare:

A grainy recording of a beheading; dash cam footage of a man being shot, execution style, in the back of the head – the title of this clip purporting it to be a Russian mob hit.

There were two bloody street fights, one of which involved someone being kicked so hard in the head that their eye had become dislodged from its socket.

Simon scrolled through the still images as well. These were usually submitted by people in the medical profession, those who had access to corpses pre-autopsy, before they were dissected, stitched and sewn, made as decent as possible for their respective tombs.

There was a picture of a man who had died from a close-range shotgun blast to the head. Another of a referee who had been decapitated and quartered after an amateur soccer match in South America had gone awry.

The next was an image of many portions of a small brown body, pieces of a young child (the sex of which was impossible to tell from the picture) who had stepped onto a landmine somewhere in one of those unfortunate places where live landmines are still a threat.

None of what he saw this Friday night compared to the footage he had captured a week prior. He knew this but wanted to confirm it for himself.

Simon scrolled until his eyes fell on his video. He was astounded to see that it had reached nearly six million views. That was far and away a record high in views for anything he had submitted. And it wasn't a number often reached on The Gore Report, not even for the clips that had been on the site far longer than his had. He imagined that, after another few weeks at this rate, his recording would crack the website's top ten most viewed videos.

Simon smiled proudly as he scrolled through the comments, nearly all of them favourable. People genuinely enjoyed his work. It made him feel better about not going out to prowl this weekend. He could rest on that video and the money he had received from it for the next little while if that's what suited him.

He was tempted to watch it again, but something stopped him. A feeling like a brief chill – here and gone but more than enough of an indication of bad weather to come. He decided he was fine with seeing only the number of views and the comments.

He exited the site feeling satisfied with his video's success. Satisfied with himself. So satisfied at the video and himself was Simon that he wanted to give himself another sort of satisfaction. With the aid of some very different videos.

He logged onto a porn streaming site. Scrolled through the recommended videos until he found something that piqued him.

Hot Pregnant Slut Fucking was the title of this piece of pornography.

He clicked play, preparing to link the clip from his phone to his TV in order to enjoy the big screen experience. Except, when the video played on his mobile device, it wasn't what he'd been expecting.

What he'd been expecting was a pregnant blonde being recorded doing the thing that had gotten her with child in the first place. What he saw was very different. So jarringly unexpected that he nearly dropped the phone from his hands.

On his phone he saw a torn and bloodied man, freshly ejected from a vehicle, crawling toward the camera, one eye clotted and ruined, the other searching aimlessly for help. Help that his congested throat would not allow him to properly ask for. Instead, he choked and gurgled his plea.

"Not again..." Simon breathed. He closed out the video. Clicked another.

Simon saw the tattered man's desperate and ruined face.

Closed out the video.

Clicked another.

He heard the gurgle, heard the wet plea for aid.

Closed the website entirely.

A glitch, a glitch, a glitch, a glitch. These words were a mantra now, something almost ritualistic. Something that Simon needed to convince himself of, because the alternative was too preposterous.

Something funny, find something funny to watch, Simon implored himself. He logged onto Netflix, clicked on one of the 80s comedies he had fallen asleep watching two days prior.

He was expecting to see Eddie Murphy and Arsenio Hall making their way to America. Instead, he saw a bloodshot eye inside a shredded face.

The tattered man's one remaining eye took up most of the screen now, and Simon knew this was not how the video was supposed to be. The eye that should have been clouded and lost seemed sharp, seemed to scan. Appeared to be looking out and around, and then... Then the pupil landed directly on Simon. His eyes meeting the one eye on the screen, locking there.

And this time it focused.

The eye.

This time it locked in on Simon like he hadn't noticed in the video before. Focused on him like it hadn't done when he'd made this recording.

Simon wanted to look away. Wanted to take his phone and throw it somewhere that was anywhere that was elsewhere.

He couldn't bring himself to do it. He was rivetted, fixated. His attention fastened and bolted to the screen in his hand.

The reddened eye was shot at such a close range that the rest of the face of the tattered man couldn't be seen.

This was not a shot he had taken, he had never zoomed in this close. Had never gotten this intimate.

The eye of the tattered man looked out of the screen at Simon, and seemingly from the eye itself came a choked and drowning noise. A single word.

"You..."

Simon let out a small sound that was something like a swallowed scream. The phone was growing hot in his hands, but he couldn't let it go, couldn't break eye contact with the speaking eye. It was entrancing him, hypnotizing him. Pulling him in. He couldn't look away. The eye, it gurgled,

"You..."

It blinked. Simon felt the movement in his bones. More urgently, he felt a burning in his hands. The phone was nearly sizzling now.

The pain in his hands broke the trance caused by the eye on the screen. He dropped the phone.

When it landed, screen down, it began to vibrate violently on the floor. Simon, wondering if it was going to explode, got up from the couch and backed away slowly.

That was when he heard it again, now coming from his television. The voice sounded stronger this time.

"You."

Simon didn't bother to look up at the larger screen. Instead, he abandoned the phone, the television, his living room. He ran into his bedroom, locking himself in there, chanting, in his mind,

A glitch, a glitch, a glitch, a glitch.

He flew into his bed, dove under his covers, rocked himself to and fro and back and forth repeating those two words to himself.

A glitch, a glitch, a glitch, a glitch.

Repeating them for nearly an entire fearful hour until he finally rocked himself to sleep.

CHAPTER SIXTEEN

Simon convinced himself it was a dream. On Saturday morning, after he woke up tangled in his sheets, sweating from nightmares he would only vaguely remember, Simon told himself that the entire episode with his phone and the video and the eye and that awful blood drenched voice was one of those (not so vague) nightmares.

Still, even with all of that convincing of his self, it took him a great deal of effort, and filled him with an unreasonable feeling of unease, to open his bedroom door and walk out into his living area. He checked the time on the display box beneath his television (which he was thankful to see was turned off), and avoided his cell phone entirely. The device was still screen-down on the area rug, reminding him of a dead body. Making it difficult for him to accept his nightmare theory.

A coincidence, he lied to himself.

The time was 11:06 AM. He had to be at Jayne's in less than an hour in order to head over to her sister's special event, which began in less than two hours.

Doing his best to forget what he was telling himself had to have been a bad dream from the night before, Simon focused only on getting ready and making sure that he and Jayne would be on time for the event. Once again, he was receiving a sense of normalcy from Jayne and was grateful that he would have her family gathering to distract him for the day. He never would have imagined himself genuinely looking forward to one of these events prior to this morning.

He wasn't yet sure what he would wear, whether or not he would be on time, or whether he would be able to enjoy himself. All Simon knew for certain on this Saturday morning was that he would be heading to the festivities minus something that had become like an extension of himself. He would be leaving his house without his phone for the first time in nearly a decade.

Content with his decision to leave his mobile device just where it was, facedown on the floor, Simon exited his apartment to head to his girlfriend's place. And then, eventually, to Jayne's sister's baby shower.

CHAPTER SEVENTEEN

"Hey... maybe you want to slow down a bit there. It's a baby shower, not a bachelor party." Jayne said to Simon as they stood in the middle of the party room in Jayne's mother's condo in downtown Toronto. Her parents had divorced when Jayne was a teenager. Her father lived halfway across the country in Alberta. The distance was his excuse to not attend events such as these. Simon, despite his earlier optimism about this gathering, wished he had an excuse similar to that of Jayne's father now that they were here in the flesh.

They were surrounded by people whom Simon had, for the last two years, learned to think of as family and friends due to Jayne's relationship with the mother-to-be. He'd tried his best to mix and mingle but found he was still rattled by the events of that week. He was conflicted. He felt naked without his phone but also wanted nothing to do with it. He was glad the device wasn't with him, though he couldn't stop thinking about it. Which is why he had been drinking himself into distraction, or at least attempting to, since they'd arrived at the party.

Simon looked at the glass of whiskey and cola in his hand. It was almost finished and he already wanted another, which would put him at number six in the two hours since they had arrived. He was a nervous drinker, and currently felt as though the bar didn't have enough booze stocked to calm him. He desperately wanted to leave. Wasn't in the mood for the fake pleasantries or the impolite questions from Jayne's family inquiring as to when he would be putting a ring on her finger, a baby in her belly. Both. Sensing his discomfort, Jayne had promised they would leave as soon as the gender reveal portion of things was over. Simon was relieved when it was announced that the reveal part of the night was about to begin.

The father and mother-to-be stood at the head of the party room on a slightly elevated stage. A large projector screen was behind them. On the screen a looping reel of photos of the couple had been playing all afternoon.

Simon could barely wait for the main event to end. His mind was full of an unwaning feeling of dread over the oddness of his recent days.

After quickly finishing his whiskey and cola, and abandoning the glass on a nearby table, Simon let Jayne know it would be his last drink of the day so long as they got out of there soon. He wasn't sure where he was in a rush to go to, he only knew that he was starting to feel suffocated surrounded by all of these people.

"Umm, I think you're butt-dialing me." Jayne said to Simon, looking curiously at her phone before showing it to him, a smile playing on her face as his name and phone number danced silently across the screen of her device.

Simon peered at the phone, unable to believe what he was seeing, knowing there was nothing in his pockets but keys and loose change. He snatched Jayne's phone from her, more desperate than he would have liked to appear. He laughed nervously to make up for the rapid and panicked movements. Looked at Jayne. Said, with a nervous tremble in his voice,

"Sorry. I kinda want to hear what my pocket has to say." He hoped he had sounded aloof, like he was joking. Though the look on Jayne's face made it clear that his performance hadn't been convincing. Ignoring her concerned expression, he answered the device, put the phone to his ear, and was unsurprised, though no less chilled, when he heard what he expected to hear.

It was the sound of someone gurgling, a sound produced by an opened throat. A gashed neck which seemed as though it was directly beside Simon's ear. Then it spoke, and he had to do all he could to stop himself from hurling the phone then and there with dozens of people all around waiting to find out if this baby would be born with a pussy or a cock.

From his phone came a blood drenched noise, a desperate gasp.

"You..."

Then a collection of clotted chokes.

"Simon..." it wheezed. It paused. It exhaled wetly, "Won't you help me, please?"

CHAPTER EIGHTEEN

Simon smiled stiffly, his body becoming rigid as it filled with his growing dread. He glanced over at Jayne to see if she had maybe heard what he had heard. She looked at him strangely. Curious. Worried. He tried to make his smile look genuine, but he found it hard to move his face. Difficult to move his arm as he disconnected the call and handed the phone back to Jayne hoping she wouldn't notice how badly his hand was trembling. Still attempting to smile, he said,

"My pocket didn't have anything important to say. But I really need to get some air, babe. I'll be back."

"Right now? They're about to do the reveal. They're shooting the gender out of a little cannon and everything. My mom worked really hard to put this all together." She sounded both wounded and annoyed.

"Yeah, I just... I just need air. Not feeling well again..." Then he turned to leave, trying not to push through the crowd the way he wanted to. Moving quickly while attempting to not seem panicked. Failing.

Simon walked toward the exit, hoping to get outside for that much-needed breath of fresh air. To clear his head and think about things logically. To rationally figure out exactly what was going on.

He was halfway to the door when he heard the soft music that had been playing over the speaker system stop abruptly, causing him to also stop abruptly on his way to the exit.

The music was replaced by what sounded like the middle of a very intimate conversation. Simon's entire being froze to the spot. He froze because it was his voice he heard, flawlessly clear, playing from the speakers all over the party room.

He only heard his voice clearly for a moment before it was soon overtaken by gasps, a shriek or two here and there, audible chatter. Then he felt their eyes.

Felt all of their eyes on his back as he wondered whether to keep walking or turn back and face them.

So many eyes, though he knew that only one eye mattered. An eye belonging to a torn and tattered face, belonging to a man now dead, yet one that still watched him. Here. Everywhere. And now it made sure that everyone could see what it could see.

Simon slowly turned around and saw the entire audience looking from the screen at the front of the party room to him. Back and forth their eyes went. Dozens of pendulums in dual sets, their judgement increasing with each oscillation.

Simon's eyes joined theirs as they looked to the screen, though he knew what he would see. Recognized the words that were coming from the speaker.

Instructions to her, from her.

He let his eyes settle with great difficultly on the video of him being intimate with his pregnant mistress. Today's woman of honour. The reason they were at this baby shower.

On the screen, Simon could be clearly seen committing what appeared, to most in attendance, to be unnatural acts along with his girlfriend's very pregnant sister.

Simon and everyone in the room – including his future in-laws, Jayne's family, Jayne – saw Simon on that big screen engaged in vulgar, milky sex (if one could call it that) with the mother-to-be.

"What the fuck!" This was a roar more so than a cohesive sentence. The father-to-be. Not pleased with this surprise pornographic video featuring his wife of less than three years. He squinted at the screen. Then, like everyone else, he turned to Simon. Roared again. A loud noise from a large man.

Simon barely heard that sound, hardly registered everything going on around him. He continued to stare at the screen after hearing his voice, her voice, their ruin.

He looked on with his heart threatening to detonate in his throat, where it had somehow gotten lodged, and where it currently thudded violently.

He broke into a cold sweat as he peeled his attention from the screen for a moment to confirm that all eyes were on him. They were.

And that was how he knew they couldn't see it.

He turned back to the video, so entranced by what he was observing that he ignored the angry mob around him.

What Simon wasn't paying attention to was the rumble of whispers and mumbles. Gasps, a few more loud exclamations.

It was easy to block them out due to the noise in his own head. Internal screams. The wailing he struggled to not let out into the party room of this condo. Because, even as he saw the video playing, witnessed himself and Jayne's sister, Sasha, covered in oil, saw his bare ass, his wet and wanting face, her gleaming naked belly, and all of their shame, he didn't care as much as he should have. It wasn't embarrassment over the lewd acts in the video that was causing him concern.

Simon didn't care that everyone had witnessed his lactophilia. Wasn't worried – even though it meant the end of his relationship, his reputation, maybe even his immediate safety – that Jayne's loved ones watched this bit of erotic lactation.

None of it mattered. None of it.

He stared at the screen. On it he saw himself on his knees in her living room, a layer of plastic sheeting all over the floor, the coffee table shoved out of the way. She was standing over him. He was treating her like a dripping faucet.

That was what everyone in the room was reacting to, he knew and understood this in a vague and far-off sort of way. What he was doing, as he looked at the screen, was trying not to shriek, hoping to not make a sound that might betray the lunacy he believed was already doing more harm to him than any of the people in the room could do, angry as they were.

Insanity, he believed, was the true fight he was up against, because what he was seeing couldn't possibly be real.

In the video displaying Jayne's sister's living room – captured by a phone he had set up on her television stand – was a third party involved in the strange passion the two central figures on the screen were in the midst of. As the Simon on the screen looked up with his mouth open, expectant, and as Sasha delivered what he was waiting for, the third figure was simply laying there, slightly behind the two, on the floor, prone. His body visible between the two of theirs. He too, leaking. His lifeblood adding to the wet works Simon and Sasha were creating on the clear, protective sheet which they were atop.

The third person in this video was laying there just as he had been after letting out his last breath when Simon had encountered him on the street a week prior. The fleshy curtains that had once been skin secured to his skull hung low, some strips touching the floor. In this video, unlike when Simon had left him on the street, he was somehow still breathing. Bubbling, more aptly. From his shredded neck came that gurgling sound, this man still attempting to belch out for help through his lacerated throat, both blood and sound spewing out. Thick ropes of his red life combined with the murky white that had already pooled on the floor to create a pinkish slurry, the sight of which was enough to make Simon want to retch. But he didn't, couldn't move. Was fixated. The sound coming from the should-be-dead man in the video, the sound playing over the speakers, was slowly driving him mad.

So consumed was Simon by this vision, and this sound no one else seemed to hear, that he missed the commotion which had broken out around him in the here and now, an earthquake emerging from the tremor of whispers and murmurs that had started when the footage had first appeared on the screen. He missed the frenzied woman screaming in anguish at her embarrassment, didn't notice her run out the door with others trailing behind her.

Simon didn't hear the heavy feet stomping toward him, nor the voices which were shouting encouragements at the owner of those feet.

Simon didn't hear or notice any of this as he stared at the screen, at the impossible man taking part in what had been one of the greatest nights of his life. A man who was staring back at Simon through one red and clouded eye. Simon didn't notice any of what was going on around him until someone stepped directly in front of him, blocking his view of the screen.

Before he could react, he felt a hand around his throat.

Then another.

Then both hands began to squeeze.

CHAPTER NINETEEN

Simon couldn't help but notice, and pay close attention, as both of these very large and strong hands which were wrapped around his neck began to cut off his air. And suddenly it was Simon in need of help yet again.

"Please! Malcolm! You don't understand..." he croaked out to Sasha's husband, the owner of the hands around his neck and a usually calm and thoughtful man, now driven wild due to an unfathomable betrayal by two people he trusted. Two people who had managed to embarrass him and his entire family – to make him question his little family-to-be – on what should have been one of the happiest days of his life.

Malcolm must have been calculating these betrayals and embarrassments because his grip tightened. Simon found that he could no longer make a sound as those same hands which had previously broken bread with him now only wished to deliver him to Death in the most intimate of fashions.

He looked around for Jayne, for Sasha, saw neither.

He looked around for their mother, hoping she would be a voice of reason. She was nowhere to be found.

He searched for help from anyone as his eyes bulged, his lungs ached, and parts of him began to grow numb. He saw many people, and they saw him, his plight. No one would come to his aid. To his overwhelming chagrin, Simon noticed that some of the people in the room were filming him. Worse, behind their phones, their cameras, he saw, on too many faces, smiles. Expressions of delight. The same morbid curiosity which drove him to routinely do just as they were doing at that moment. He didn't blame them. In fact, he was thankful for the reminder. When life went sour, turned violent, became unfortunate, most people were either witnesses or victims, with very few heroes in between. Everyone in this world, when it comes down to it, is on their own.

He kicked up as hard as he could, caught Malcolm directly in the testicles with his shin. His brother-in-law-to-be went down instantly. Tried to reach out for Simon, but his body wouldn't allow him to as it attempted to recover from a pain that felt like a battering ram had hit him in the genitals and stomach.

Simon reeled, drawing breath, trying to regain his composure and his bearings as he did so.

Suddenly, those who had been witnesses sprang into action. Several in the crowd who had been watching or filming or both began to move forward. Whether they were moving to help Malcolm or to finish what he had started, Simon didn't know. Didn't want to find out.

He turned on very shaky legs and found the strength to run to the exit and out of the building.

CHAPTER TWENTY

Simon didn't make it far after heading out the front door. He had run from one bitter confrontation to another.

In front of the building, and to the delight of a growing crowd (many of whom had their phones out, filming), was a very pregnant Sasha being screamed at by a sobbing, wildly frustrated Jayne, their mother between them, looking as though she was worried that things might get physical despite her older daughter's condition. All three women were crying and trying to talk over each other. Jayne's voice was so clotted with tears that Simon couldn't make out what she was saying. Though he didn't need to decipher the words to understand that they were nothing good. Not for them. Not for him.

He stopped.

They stopped when they noticed him stopping. All three women turned their full attention to him, which made the entire audience turn to him. More cameras, more witnesses hoping to give those who could not be here to see things firsthand an opportunity to witness along with them. Vicarious living.

Simon thought of the live feeds he could be on at that very moment. Facebook, Instagram, every social media platform. Those who weren't going live at that moment would go back home, send these videos to friends, upload them to YouTube, share them indiscriminately everywhere.

Simon pictured reactions of laughter all over the world at his expense. It was too much for him to handle.

"You fucking asshole!" Jayne shouted. Simon heard that very clearly.

"Look, baby." His head was cloudy from the whiskey and the choking. "Let me explain. I just... I have a thing for..."

He stopped. Looked at Sasha, who would not look at him or anyone, her head hanging low. One might have thought she was admiring her growing belly and the baby within it, but she slowly shook her head, back and forth and back and forth, contemplating what her and her baby's lives would be like from this point on.

Simon didn't dare look at Jayne's mother.

"What?" Jayne shrieked. And the attention once again was all hers. "You have a thing for my sister? For *breast milk*! Which one? Jesus Christ, you really are a fucking freak."

The crowd erupted at this, now fully understanding the scene unfolding in front of them. Gasps, laughs, jeers, all manner of chatter.

Simon went to speak, but Jayne's eyes flashed at him as if she had suddenly remembered something. It was a look that stopped whatever words he would have said from reaching any ears. Simon believed he knew exactly what it was that she had remembered. And he wasn't incorrect.

"Oh my God! Did you *sell* those videos of you and my sister?"

Oohs and ahhs and expletives from the ever-growing audience. Some people joined the crowd from inside the condo where the baby shower was being held, others were drawn in from all areas along the bustling downtown street.

Jayne's question caused Sasha to finally look up, her eyes red, anguished, shamed. And now, a new emotion was clear in those eyes, one that she hadn't expected to experience after all she had done. It was betrayal.

VIRAL LIVES

"*What*? You sold videos of me? Tell me that's not true, Simon! Tell me you wouldn't do that! Oh Jesus Christ... Holy fuck, my life is over..." Then Sasha sank to the ground and her mother, somewhat hesitantly, leaned over and awkwardly consoled her, patting her shoulder while looking scornfully at Simon.

"No." Simon said. He repeated "No!" The second time with more conviction. But the world was closing in on him. There were too many people around, too many smiling faces, too many strangers drawing their entertainment from this. He wanted to continue to deny that he had sold perhaps a few well edited and appropriately scrambled clips of his trysts with Sasha over the months, but he knew it was no use. And he didn't want this audience here to see him make a fool of himself. Besides, there was the matter of Malcolm and many angry others who could still be coming after Simon at that moment. People who were not interested in hearing anything from him other than noises indicative of physical pain.

For the second time in a few minutes, Simon's mind, not long from being oxygen deprived, told him to run. He intended to do just that.

"I'm sorry," he said to Jayne. To them all, "I'm sorry!"

Then he covered his face from the witnesses (and those who witnessed vicariously through them) and he ran. Not sure where he was going, just knowing he had to get away from here. He would call Jayne as soon as he had access to a phone he could trust. He would try to explain everything to her, beg her to come back. Tell her he had a problem. Several. She would forgive him, she had to. That was what he thought. Hoped.

He pushed his way through the crowd, taking a modicum of pleasure in knocking the phone out of one bystander's hands. Loved the sound of it crashing to the sidewalk. He stepped off of that sidewalk, into the road.

"Simon! Get back here!" He heard but ignored Jayne's voice as he made his way across the road. Then he heard her say,

"Simon! Look out!"

Perhaps he should have ignored this as well. Because what he did, instead of continuing his dizzy run across the street, was stop and look out.

Simon didn't like what he saw. But wasn't given much time to process just how much he disliked it.

There was the screech of peeling tires.

A honking horn.

A sudden crash.

A dented car.

A broken man.

Simon, after having been sent flying over the entire length of the car and landing directly on the side of his head, was still aware.

Laying there, on his back, on the street, bleeding out, he looked for the vehicle which had just struck him. A purple muscle car was there, idling for a moment. Then, in broad daylight, it sped off.

Simon smiled bitterly, or at least attempted to. He didn't blame the driver. Not in the least. There were so many eyes, so many judging, accusing eyes. Not to mention the cameras everywhere. He wanted to be out of here just as badly. And perhaps, he realized as he went to move extremities that now refused to respond, he would be out of here sooner than he had ever expected to be.

Simon began to cry. Not because of the pain, but because he didn't feel any pain. He felt nothing from the neck down. And what he could feel, at the back of his head, didn't feel promising. His own blood pooled beneath him, leaking from where his skull had cracked.

"Simon!" Jayne screamed out, and she ran to his side. Simon took a small measure of relief in this. There was pain in her voice, hurt as well. But the love was still there. Maybe, if he made it out of this alive, he hoped, as his mind threatened to fade, just maybe they could work things out.

"Simon, are you okay?"

He tried to answer but couldn't. When he went to speak, he noticed that his words were wet, were absorbed by the blood which was running out of his mouth, covering his lips and chin. He only looked at her, hoping that he could relay to her that he did love her despite his depravities with her sister. Jayne was the most understanding person he had ever met. The most trusting. Had kept the secret of his part-time profession when most women would have run for the hills immediately. He loved her dearly for that, and only wished he could tell her so. Though, even if he could speak, she wouldn't have heard him over the din and clamour. Over the onlookers in the street who were all shouting instructions on whether or not to touch him, who to call, what to do. The entire time, so many of them filmed.

Simon saw this as he looked into the crowd. Heard the world grow louder as everyone who had been inside the party room, along with residents of the condo, began to spill out of the building until the sidewalk and most of the street was filled with humanity, all circling Simon's crumpled body, none wanting to touch his twisted frame. A body which now had so many broken, oddly angled parts.

Simon watched them watch him. Saw the cameras, knew his fate, understood but hated every one of them just the same.

He needed help. Why was no one helping?

He saw that some of them were actually on their phones rather than just watching from behind them. Simon took that as a good sign that maybe someone was calling for an ambulance.

After struggling to push through the crowd, Jayne's mother approached Simon. Not to assist, but to pull Jayne away.

"You can't touch him, you might make it worse. Help is on the way." she informed her daughter, trying her best to keep her voice calm.

Simon attempted to smile at this, even while he felt as though something had been ripped out of him as Jayne and her mother went back toward the crowd, joining the gathered onlookers, Jayne wailing the entire time, her mother attempting to give her what comfort she could.

To Simon's growing dismay, no one seemed to want to go near him.

He tried to look down at his body, tried to see why Jayne's mother was so terrified to touch him, but he couldn't raise or turn his head from where it was positioned, gazing to his left at the spectators standing outside of the condo entrance.

He blinked away tears, the crowd growing fuzzy as he did so. Then, after he gave up the blinking and allowed the tears to flow, to run their course, the crowd became clear again.

That was when he saw someone he hadn't noticed there a moment before. Someone he was certain hadn't been there a moment before. Someone that stood in the crowd and stood out amongst them. And when this person saw Simon see him, he smiled, and Simon saw a glint inside of his mouth. Something shining that he couldn't identify.

Simon wanted to look for Jayne, for Sasha, for any face other than this one, but he couldn't take his eyes off of this man. Even in his woe, Simon couldn't help but be in awe of this man's unearthly beauty. And, as if recognizing this, the man stepped forward and approached Simon while no one else would.

At first, when Simon had seen this man, he'd thought this was the help which had been called for. The man wore a white trench coat, and Simon first mistook it for a doctor's smock. Thought he had been lucky enough to have drawn the attention of some doctor on duty nearby. But the jacket wasn't right. It was too bright. It gleamed loudly, glowing brighter than the day around them.

Simon tried to raise his hand to shield his eyes but remembered that his body was useless. He could only watch, squinting as this Shining Stranger, this far too handsome black man dressed in a far too bright white coat, stepped towards him. Walked over until he was standing nearly atop of Simon.

Simon called out to this stranger for help. Or at least he tried to. The sound that actually came out of him was,

"Hrlghrl."

A gurgle.

The stranger only continued to smile down at Simon, his coat nearly blinding the dying man. Simon was certain then that this had to be an angel. An apparition sent to take him to the other side.

He was about to take solace in this until he saw the Walking Angel reach into one of his pockets and retrieve from it a recording device. Not a cellphone like so many of the others held and used as they stood in the crowd waiting for help that would be too late, recording this man die. Instead, the stranger produced a camcorder, what looked like something from the 90's. Large and gaudy. Simon couldn't understand how it could have fit into the man's coat.

Simon's eyes and lips began to move rapidly – this was him trying to run off, to cover his face, to push the man and his camcorder away, but no part of his body would respond except for the muscles in his face. He went nowhere. And had to watch this man begin to record him.

He tried to ask 'why?', but he only emitted another gurgle. Yet, somehow, the man standing over him recording seemed to understand. Because he parted his lips in response. Another glint of something shining sparkled from between them.

"Eventually," The Black Man In The White Trench Coat said, "you'll understand."

Then he stepped out of Simon's immediate view, though not before nodding in the direction of the crowd he had emerged from.

Simon was able to shift his eyes to look where the stranger had indicated. It took nearly all his strength at this point to simply roll his eyes back in that direction. When he did, he was initially confused, seeing nothing but those same witnesses. Seeing faces, some curious, some concerned, looking back at him.

He was going to attempt to say to The Shining Stranger that he didn't understand, but that was when his eyes drifted downward. To the feet, not the faces.

Simon saw something then that made his eyes open and close and roll around in his head wildly, his lips contort, his face twist into a picture of grief.

He saw a hand, bloodied, reaching through a pair of legs. Witnessed an arm behind that reddened hand as someone was crawling their way out of the gathered group.

Saw the face belonging to that hand and arm emerge from between two legs as this person dragged himself under and through the mass of witnesses. Simon's mind reeled as he observed this familiar man pulling his ruined body off of the sidewalk and onto the street, getting closer to Simon.

Crawling, the skin on his face like stripped and hanging meat drying in the sun.

One of his eyes was clotted with blood, the other stared out dimly, but intently. That one bloodred eye had only a single thing in its focus.

Simon.

Simon who lay there unable to move, though he desperately tried to as the tattered man neared him, crawling slowly, his seeing eye eager, his hand reaching, reaching, then touching Simon's face – a collection of burning brimstone making contact with his skin.

Simon's eyes flared wide open, he let out a wet scream, cried out indecipherably for help.

It was the last thing he did, the last sound his audience would ever hear from him as his soul escaped his body. Though it was far from the last time the sound would be heard.

The Black Man In The White Trench Coat looked down at the husk of Simon Hinch, calmly put the camcorder back in his pocket, and walked away.

POST-MORTEM

The video was an instant classic on every gore site – The Gore Report, Moment of Death, Gorey Stories – all of them uploaded the multiple videos they received of the death of the unfortune man who would forevermore only be known across the internet by one of several headlines, including, but not limited to:

'INSTANT KARMA: CHEATING BOYFRIEND GETS KILLED IN HIT AND RUN'

'THE CIRCLE OF LIFE: MAN DIES AT MISTRESS'S BABY SHOWER'

'JAY WALKER HIT BY CAR'

'MAN ENDS HIS LIFE WHEN HIS SECRETS ARE EXPOSED'

Every website had its own spin on the videos, but only one site – The Gore Report – had received the footage that truly inflamed the internet. The video showing a perspective of the dying man none of the other recordings could justify.

None of the many clips of Simon's death which had made the rounds on the web had shown anyone taking a video of the dying man from directly above him, yet this one version of Simon's death was shot as though someone had been recording while standing nearly overtop of him.

This video had been sent to The Gore Report anonymously through standard mail. Oddly enough, it had been recorded on a VHS cassette with no description and no return address, not even a suggested title, which most submitters usually made sure to give.

After tracking down the outdated pieces of technology that would allow him to play and convert the video, Mr. Rood, the owner of The Gore Report, only had to watch the recording once before coming up with the title that would truly shake up the internet:

'MAN RECOGNIZES DEATH BEFORE IT TAKES HIM'

He uploaded the converted recording immediately. And immediately it was a success.

This video garnered millions of views within the first day of its release. Then millions more daily as people dissected it in comparison with the other videos showing Simon's death. They examined this perspective in relation to the rest. They talked for years about the look in the man's eyes before he died. It had been a look of sheer insanity.

Then he had screamed. Tried to. What had come out was a gurgling sound that was the icing on the cake for those who enjoyed such grimly decorated desserts.

Some would masturbate to this sound, to the video, to Simon's death. Others would share it with friends as proof of one belief or another. The debates raged on over who or what the man had been mumbling to as he lay there dying in the street, and why he had tried to cry out before his end.

The comments sections were wild.

Many people simply regarded and appreciated it for what it was: snuff. Which is why they didn't bother trying to dissect the video. Because these viewers, deep down, understood that sometimes people just want to watch other people die. They had no qualms about their pleasures.

So, they watched. They reacted. They shared. And those whom they shared with repeated the process. None of them knowing that each time – every single time the video was played – Simon, or at least his soul, would have to relive it again. Would feel the reactions, hear the comments, die once more.

And then repeat. Repeated for each of the millions of views, and each of the millions to come, for all of the viewers who watched.

Because of them, Simon Hinch would perpetually relive the end of his life, always desperately crying out for help. Help that was far beyond him.

Thanks For Reading!

Gore websites have been around for a very long time, some getting over a billion views per month. There has been at least one murderer caught after uploading his heinous crimes onto one of these sites.

Some argue that these types of sites help prevent people from going out and doing gruesome acts themselves, others say these sites only encourage people to want to personally experience the real thing. I've never understood the fascination, but I thought it was worth exploring in fiction. I hope you found it interesting.

Whether or not you did, I hope you take the time to rate and review this novella, and let the humans on Goodreads, Amazon, and those who follow you on your social media platforms, know your thoughts. As always, every review truly helps, and I appreciate them all.

I would like to quickly acknowledge my editor Alessandra Sztrimbely for her corrections and perspective. Also, Courtney Swank for her constant help with my releases. And my brother, Fred, who, in my heart, I dedicate everything I write to. Also, you, the readers, the people who support my work. I am profoundly grateful that your eyes are on these words right now. Thank you kindly.

Stay tuned for more madness.

-Dimaro

HERE'S A PREVIEW OF THINGS TO COME...

In order to save the future, they must bring forward one of the greatest evils of the past.

2222

A Novel (With Graphics)

Coming Early 2021

IN ORDER TO SAVE THE FUTURE, THEY MUST BRING
FORWARD ONE OF THE GREATEST EVILS OF THE PAST.

FELIX I.D. DIMARO

AUTHOR OF "BUG SPRAY: A TALE OF MADNESS" AND "HOW TO MAKE A MONSTER"

1945

THE
BEGGING
BEAST

HOW MUCH MORE GRIEVOUS ARE THE
CONSEQUENCES OF ANGER THAN THE
CAUSES OF IT.
— MARCUS AURELIUS

BERLIN, GERMANY
APRIL 30, 1945
SHORTLY AFTER 1 PM

All of a sudden, he was in the mood for murder. He had his gun out. It was leveled at the man before him. In front of him, this man, whose uniform was pressed and in pristine order, the medals on his chest declaring his bravery, his honour, this man cowered. Begged.

The man with the gun saw these medals and the lies they represented and wanted to spit. Wanted to do much more than that. And the person he had his pistol aimed at knew it. He was standing with his hands out in front of him, trembling, palms up, showing that he had no intention of reaching for the pistol at his hip, pleading instead for this not to happen. This vile and lowly begging man. No, not a man, the one holding the gun thought to himself. Not a person, but a beast.

A monster dressed in human skin.

This monster fell to his knees and began to plead more fervently.

"No!" he screamed as he dragged himself backward on the floor, toward a pale yellow patterned couch. A couch upon which sat, slumped, the dead body of the uniformed tyrant's wife.

He backed up until he hit the couch. His head swivelling around violently as if looking for a place to go, wanting to be anywhere but here, in front of this large, dark man holding what seemed to be an even larger and darker and unwavering gun.

The man holding the gun was conflicted. He knew his instructions were to go back to this point in time and get this creature. Emphasis on 'get'. The second half of those instructions had been 'do not harm him, whatsoever', emphasis on all of those words. But now, as he was in the process of completing his task – the mission he had worked toward for the last two years, the assignment that would get him back his family, get him an actual life – all he wanted to do was shoot Adolf Hitler in the face.

It would take a second. And, yes, it would change everything for them. It might even mean the end of him. But he was a soldier, a man of sacrifice. He, his team, so many others, would be happy to sacrifice themselves if it meant their time hadn't wound up the way their time had wound up. Nutrient patches instead of food, man-made islands where bodies were piled atop each other and told to live that way, and the never-ending conflict that this monster had championed, still felt even three hundred years later. Desmond could end it all, the pain and suffering – maybe – if he pulled the trigger right then and there...

He made his decision. Gun leveled at the monster's head, Desmond Drew walked over to Hitler...

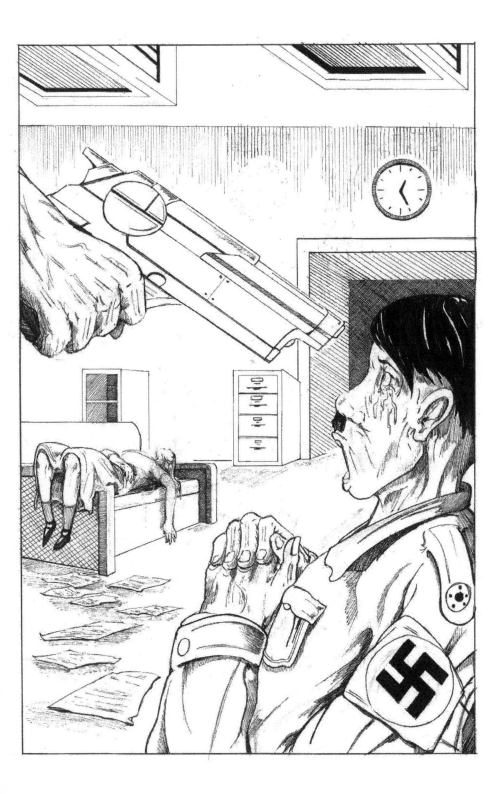

Made in the USA
Columbia, SC
15 January 2021